"Enough!" Kantsky said…

The display flashed a brief message: "Warning: Cabin Pressure Change. Please attach backup breathing apparatus."

Dammit, I thought. If there was a backup breathing apparatus I had no time to find it. I was seized with sudden vertigo, overcome with dizziness, and I passed out. As I did the edges of reality perforated with red static, making me think for a moment my eyes were bleeding…

THE GOBO BRIDE

OTHER SPECULATIVE FICTION
FROM SIDEWALK LABS

Day Trips, by Curt Cannon et al.
Elisha Morgan, by Curt Cannon
Riches, by Martin Embers
Aaron Robertson's Sycamore, by Louis Charles
The Eye of Set, by G.S. Christopher
The Isle of Dreams, by Martin Embers

A Lewis Gregory Mystery

The Gobo Bride

MASON ADGETT

A Sidewalk Labs Creation.
Palm Bay, FL, USA.

Copyright © 2019 by Mason Adgett and Sidewalk Labs Creations.

All rights reserved. Printed in the United States of America. No part of this book may be reproduced without the written permission of Sidewalk Labs, except in the case of brief quotations in critical articles and reviews.

For information about this work and other Sidewalk Labs Creations contact:
publisher@sidewalklabs.net
or visit
www.sidewalklabs.net

First Edition v1.
November 2019.

ISBN: 978-0-9980770-2-4

·····1·····

I WAS WATCHING A NEWS ARTICLE on the wall 3V when I got the call from my brother on my cell. I paused the V and patted my cell onto my lash. When the image focused I could see he was in his office. I recognized the huge painting of Beethoven that hung behind his chair. I couldn't see him, just the painting, which meant he hadn't even bothered to put the cell on his eye, just left it sitting there on the desk.

"Hey, did you see the show this week?" he said.

The show he meant was *Lewis Gregory, Private Investigator*. Due to the surprise success of his new reality feed, my brother Lewis had recently become the most famous private detective in the Dallas-Houston polyplex. I hated his show – I considered it an embarrassment to the Gregory name – but I didn't have the heart to tell him so.

Anyway if I did it would have done damage to my income. Lewis wasn't just family, he was also my most frequent employer (among too many) and so it would hardly have been in my best interest to avoid taking part in his newest enterprise. But it was not my favorite gig. I hate publicity, I'm not fond of souped-up reality feeds, I don't like being noticed, and nowadays working for Lewis meant having a 3V crew constantly at my back.

Still I answered the phone because there was a good chance there was a job in it and I needed the jobs to come as frequently as the bills did.

"I haven't watched it yet," I said. I hadn't intended to.

"I'm going to send it to you," he said. A moment later his shoulder appeared in the picture, then my cell pinged and a notification flew by my peripheral vision. I swiped it off-screen.

"I'm watching the news," I said. "You do realize how close we are to electing this ass, right?"

"Who?" he said. "Curry?"

I sighed. "No one is going to vote for Curry. I mean Krumb." I personally didn't think he was civilized enough for the position of Earth's Arbiter of Civilization.

"Yeah," he said. "He's got Darby's vote."

"You're not voting for him, are you?" I asked, appalled.

"I'm not voting," he said. "You can't trust any of them. It's all rigged. Civilization will pick whoever they want and say we did it. I don't know why you even worry about politics. Have you at least heard who I had on the show? It's not like you've filtered me out of your feed." He laughed, then paused uncomfortably, then laughed again. "It got over ten million replays in the first hour."

"Great," I said. "That's really great. I'm proud of you."

"Just turn it on," he pleaded.

I rolled my eyes — figuring he wasn't looking at his screen anyway — and flicked towards the wall to replace the news with my cell display. I tapped my temple to pull up my messages. His was the only one unread since I was fairly religious about keeping up with my communications.

"Do I have to watch the whole thing now?" I asked. "Or can I start it in the middle?"

He stood up and put his cell on solely so he could give me a wounded look and see if I felt any shame. I didn't.

"Just watch it," he said. But now that I could see him I took a moment to admire his hat. I couldn't see the top of it, it just kept going and going like the electric rabbit. In a rare moment of acuity he read my expression and touched the metal brim of it proudly. "Do you like it? It's a Wurlit Top Popper."

"Obviously," I said.

"Pretty neat, right? It's a hologram. Goes as high as the ceiling if I want."

"I'm sure you stand out in a crowd."

"I know," he beamed.

I hit play on the video and pushed the slider past the credits, then shoved another three minutes or so out of the way for good measure and ended up in the middle of an argument between Lewis and his full-time assistant and bodyguard Mike. I jumped another thirty seconds because I don't like drama. Now I was in the middle of Lewis telling the audience how he liked to work. He gave no specifics but repeated his favorite phrase a few times, "from the outside, in." Yep, that's how Lewis worked: "from the outside, in." Emphasis on the comma.

Don't try to work out what it means. Having known Lewis his whole life, I can promise you it means nothing. He acted like he really believed "outside, in" represented some kind of method but I suspect he knew better which is why he called me in anytime things got even remotely complicated. "Legwork," he called it but it really meant "watch my back and make sure I don't screw this up."

When I pushed another minute into the video I realized why he had called me. A close-up filled the screen, a face I recognized immediately. Anyone would have: India Phoenix, celebrity socialite, heiress, society ingénue. She was one of those rich celebrity girls who didn't do anything at all but still everybody constantly needed to know what she was doing.

"Keep watching," Lewis said. "She'll come on in a minute."

"You mean India?" I said.

"You skipped ahead!" he objected.

The video cut to show her full entourage: two beefy security guards and an old lady in a purple skinsuit with a hat to rival Lewis's, only hers was no hologram. They were all seated in the luxury couch that curled around his desk. "She's a client?"

"Just listen to it," he said.

So I turned my attention back to the video. The camera stayed on India – a good choice – but it was the old lady who was talking. I listened with one ear while my eyes took in Phoenix. She wore a satiny robe with a black lace fringe that clung to her curves, highlighted by some kind of accentuator that created a soft glow where it touched bare skin. It probably cost more than my entire life up to this point.

She was way more attractive than she deserved, I thought. Despite her looks I had never really liked her. She came from the kind of centuries-old money I despised and she always wore a pouty half-frown like someone had stolen a lick of her ice cream. Hers was probably the most famous pout in the solar system.

Anyway, the old lady was saying, "We trust him, of course. But a family such as ours must protect its interests."

The video cut to Lewis, who nodded. "Of course, of course. The integrity of your name."

"We must be very cautious about our connections," the old lady said. "Vavaka loves India deeply but any time two such important families unite business interests can become complicated."

I paused the vid. "Okay," I said to Lewis, "I knew she was getting married. She's hiring *you*? To do what, investigate his family?"

"Background," he said.

"She's marrying an alien," I said, thinking aloud, repeating something I had only recently heard. I skipped most gossip vids but it was a trending topic even in the news. I just hadn't realized the info had come from Lewis's show.

"Gobo," he said. "It's a gobo. You know gobos?"

I was somewhat familiar. "With the funny eyelids," I said.

"His name's Vavaka. He owns U-Ship."

That was something. Since U-Ship was the largest shipping company on Earth I had always figured it was

Earth-based. Just goes to show there's a lot I don't know. I had rented their hover-trucks the last two times I had moved but all I knew about them was the single day price for a three meter glider: $318.

I knew only slightly more about gobos in general, who had started to show up on Earth pretty commonly in the last five years or so. Asitot was about ten years behind us in star-travel. I paid a lot of attention to alien immigration, especially when it came to nucleites (organisms evolved on the nucleotide), not because I was worried about an alien takeover – many still feared such things – but because I was fascinated by the variety of human-like life that cropped up in all corners of the universe. Not all nucleites were human-like, of course, just like all animals don't necessarily have arms, legs, or eyeballs. What I found intriguing was the homogeny of the variety – if such an oxymoron may be considered – in that where there were nucleites there were primates and arachnids and amphibians and cetera. I read all the writings of the higher organisms on the subject as soon as they were translated, which didn't happen as often as you might think in a universe so vast. Since nucleites struggle with the complexity of languages used among the completely different hive-like and trans-dimensional minds of bosonites and leptonites their work hardly ever makes it down to the lower languages. Humans, a tier-4 nucleite, don't even really have a reason to read the philosophies of, say, the Copwul meld system, which I think is considered a single tier 3 bosonite. I know I should probably leave these distinctions to scientists and if any such are reading this I apologize. I may have mixed up the Kent-

Stark classifications levels.

Anyway, I said to Lewis, "You're going to Asitot?"

He said, "Well..."

And there it was. You didn't have to square *r* and multiply by *pi* to draw a circle around where he was headed. Lewis leave Earth? You could barely get him to leave Houston.

"So," I said. "You want me to go to a distant star that I've never been to and dig up dirt on a powerfully connected alien at the request of some celebrity rich kid."

"It's India Phoenix!" he said.

He did have a point. Honestly it sounded right up my alley.

For fifteen minutes we haggled over my pay — I felt I was worth at least as much as a U-Ship hover glider. We settled on slightly higher per diem and I agreed to take the case.

....2....

REALITY 3V SHOWS ARE NOT GENERALLY AS REAL as they would have you believe. Was Lewis a real private detective? Yes. Were the events shown in the feed real events that transpired in his life? To a degree. But most of what was shown were re-enactments and souped-up stagings of things that had already taken place.

That was the thing that bothered me most about working with Lewis nowadays: all the acting.

I met with India Phoenix the next day, January 14, 2166 (a Tuesday). We talked initially for about twenty minutes, all of it recorded on multiple video streams. India wanted to play it back right away (as did Lewis) so we sat through that. This led to all kinds of "great ideas." India – who as one of the premiere body actresses on Earth was certainly no stranger to constructed entertainment – was game for another shoot and re-writes were managed on the fly by India's manager (the old lady from the video) and Lewis with occasional input from India. I kept my thoughts to myself and delivered all my lines as I usually do – dry with an emphasis on diction. Lewis tried to get me worked up to no avail.

"People like drama," he said and behind him Debra Rhine, the manager, nodded emphatically. I was sure I wasn't the only exception to this rule. I said so and India laughed.

"Let him be a stick," she said. "It's good contrast."

"Of course," said Lewis. With India he was all deference and courtesy, a little on the groveling side if you ask me. But any man could be forgiven it considering the snug way she fit into iridescent stretch pants. The bright red cloth drew immediate attention to her well-rounded assets.

It became obvious that the reason they hired Lewis was the opportunity to be on the show. They wanted our investigation to appear before a wide audience. India Phoenix clearly loved the spotlight but I thought there had to be more to it than that. How, I wondered, did a powerful gobo like Vavaka feel about all the publicity? But when I asked about it in the initial interview they brushed the question aside.

"Both India and Vavaka are big fans," Ms. Rhine said. "Also we reserve the right to review all footage first."

"It's in the contract," said Lewis.

"You mean even if I find something we might not show it," I said.

"Right," she said. "Depending on what it is."

That was standard reality 3V. Every client reserved the right for confidentiality and more than half never shared what was discovered. I wondered what was the point of asking me to dig up Vavaka's dirty laundry on such a public medium if they didn't want me to display it? But I figured the rich would do anything for

13

publicity's sake. All the attention was good for branding both for the Phoenix label and for Vavaka and apparently the Lewis Gregory show was taking off on Asitot in a big way.

The whole interview took place with four members of a video crew crouching in various corners and talking between takes about things like compensation for stereoscopic drift and light temperature adjustments. One of them, the polygonist, used a cad-cam to detail all the objects in the room, including the people. I asked him if my face had changed much since our last shoot. He said, "You're grayer and you're fatter." I was a fit twenty-six. I couldn't tell if he was joking or if he didn't like me.

Anyway, I got the facts of the case in twenty minutes, then we filmed for another five hours. Here are those facts, sans re-takes:

India Phoenix and Vavaka as'Tatim first met four years prior at the virtual premiere of the game Galactic Empires. I knew it well. It had exploded in popularity since and I personally wasted far too much of my life on the DNA Wars expansion pack. India and Vavaka hit it off immediately (though India was at that time only sixteen) and met again for several play dates over the next year.

It was funny, India said, that at the premiere she had modded gobo while he had modded human and they only later realized the coincidence when they were comfortable enough to talk about their backgrounds.

A year ago their relationship had become – as India put it – a "matter of state" when Vavaka had casually brought up the possibility of marriage. It was a bit of a surprise as they had yet to meet face to face but after considering it she found she rather liked the idea. Such relationships today were common. It was her family who was old-fashioned, she felt. Vavaka, she said, was fun. He had a sense of humor. He was competitive in all the right ways. Charming and considerate. Her only complaint was his lack of time as he oversaw most of his business interests personally. Which she also admired.

But if his proposal was a surprise to her it was even more so to the Phoenix family. Who was this alien? Where in the universe was this planet Asitot? How long had they been communicating? The most important question: how would this association with an alien affect the Phoenix family name?

"My family doesn't really know much about the rest of the universe," she said with a shrug. Most people didn't. It was too big to keep track of so hardly anyone bothered.

"But you were fascinated by it, no doubt," I helped out.

"What do you mean?"

"That he is alien. Not human."

"He's different," she said. "I like different."

None of that particular dialogue made it into the final version. Instead India ran over his virtues again, the beginning of a refinement that wouldn't be perfect until somewhere around take 18. Then she explained how after Ms. Rhine's connections had looked into his business matters their skepticism had turned to growing support. Still they had decided to keep the relationship private, waiting to reveal it until they came to Lewis and asked to appear on the show. They both watched it, both were big fans, both thought it would be "fun." India was defined, apparently, by "fun." That was when I first delicately probed about the consequences of finding something embarrassing, still not sure why they would request an official investigation – and from all I could tell they meant it to be legitimate – on such a public forum. They answered in one take, cut from the final episode:

Ms. Rhine: "We expect you will discover nothing untoward. In any case you will update us regularly."

Lewis: "Of course."

Ms. Rhine: "We will provide all capturing equipment. All material will be uploaded to us at the end of the working day. We will review all recordings before release to your production team."

Lewis: "Absolutely."

Ms. Rhine: "Anything unexpected you find concerning Vavaka as'Tatim you will reveal directly to me."

India: "And me."

These words were all accompanied with a heavy sort of eye contact that I believe was supposed to command my very soul but it was Lewis who answered, "No doubt about it." He then favored me with his own weaker version of the hypnotic gaze and said, "That was all prepared in the contract."

I nodded and went on with the interview. The wedding would take place in March, two months away. India would travel immediately to Asitot where she would meet Vavaka face to face for the first time. I would accompany her and once on Asitot I would begin investigations into her fiancé's background while she began wedding preparations in the traditional style of Asitot, as per Vavaka's request.

It didn't give me much time to prepare but to tell the truth I was keen to get started. I kept my excitement hidden, in my usual style, but an all-expenses paid trip to a recently unveiled nucleite bred planet felt like winning the lottery to me. As it also meant two days travel time with the incredibly beautiful India Phoenix, I agreed to be ready to leave the next morning.

To prepare I questioned her about Asitot and gobos in general. It was astonishing how little she seemed to know considering she was prepared to marry one.

"What I always liked about them," she said, "what attracted me to them right away was their eyes, you know, how large and colorful they are? I thought it was crazy how many different colors they had, and the textures?" The way India talked you got the impression her head was full of questions more than statements. "You know what I'm talking about? They have all these different eyelids."

I did know what she was talking about. It was the feature that most distinguished gobos from humans. Each gobo had a unique set of eye-filters behind a fully opaque outer membrane. Humans thought of them as extra eyelids as they often appeared that way from the outside but they were much thinner, a different material entirely, designed to filter light in various ways. There were thousands of varieties scattered across the gene pool. An individual gobo could have anywhere from five to fifteen of these filters on average. I had read about it and watched several detailed videos the night before, fascinated by this strange deoxyribonucleic variation.

India said, "That's why I wanted to mod one for the premiere. You know that was the first release you could do the sensory immersion? That was so fun. Have you done that?"

I had indeed tried sensory immersion. In fact I tried it every time I felt flush enough to afford it. I had extended my credit a little the previous night to experience the gobo vision mod myself.

"It's not perfect." I said. "It's just a simulation." Since a human brain wasn't wired the same there was no way to truly replicate the gobo experience. Part of the reason gobos had the extra filters was the incredible sensitivity of their vision which extended well into the infra-red and ultraviolet spectrums. Ours was, as I told her, a much reduced experience.

"You're no fun," she said. "It seemed pretty real to me."

"What can you tell me about the culture?" I asked.

She shrugged. "I know Vav likes to game," she said. "Everybody on Asitot plays *Empires*. I can't wait to get in and start decorating. I've simmed the city a bunch of times, the house too. You know Jebala, where his estate his?"

"You're going to live on Asitot?"

"For a bit." She seemed unconcerned by the idea. "I'll probably travel a lot."

"What about your career?" I asked. "You intend to keep working?"

"Oh!" she said, like a big idea had just occurred to her. "They *love* old movies on Barnaby. I should be able to get a lot of work there."

Barnaby was Asitot's inhabited moon.

"But you don't intend to live on Barnaby, correct?" I asked.

"It's all Pyramus," she said, and about the same time, Ms. Rhine interjected:

"Is this line of questioning necessary?"

Which was of course an indication to Lewis that it wasn't so I cut it short. I didn't mention what I had already learned on my own about the Pyramus star system. Sure Asitot and Barnaby were both gobo (*guvian* I understand is the proper term) but politically they had split about 150 years ago quite harshly. Living on Asitot and working on Pyramus? From what I had gathered that would not be a simple prospect.

By the end of the interview I felt a condescending sympathy for India Phoenix who by all social measures was far better off than I but who seemed to be swimming into waters a little above her head. She failed, I thought, to appreciate the vast difference between humans and other aliens, as did her agent, advisor, or whatever function Ms. Rhine served. It wasn't my business, however, to protect the Phoenix family from itself — just from any improper or illegal machinations of those wishing to align themselves with them.

The whole time we talked India was continually distracted by her cell, so much so that Ms. Rhine threatened to make her stop wearing it. We had to re-shoot several conversations, though the polygonist assured us he would be able to remove the cell in post anyway. That kind of trick was easy enough my own cell's camera had it built in. People hardly ever took their cells off their eyes anymore but they still wanted their selfies to be free of the distraction.

"Important conversation?" I asked once when India had that look that people got when they were having a real dialogue face to face but were really spending most of the time thinking about the message they were formulating for a private chat window. "Vavaka?" I guessed.

She hesitated. "No, it's nothing."

Ms. Rhine gave her a sharp look but didn't press the issue. It wasn't until much later as I was leaving that I had an opportunity to bring it up with India. As the video crew wrapped up in Lewis's office we were alone for a few minutes in the foyer.

"You look worried," I said.

Her eyes darted to mine then back into that inner space reserved for cell phone operation then to mine again. "There is this person," she said as though dismissing it, but then followed it up with a more earnest tone: "Some kind of crazy fan?"

"A man?" I said. "A human?"

She shrugged. "I suppose so, yes. Someone I've gamed with, probably."

Her voice had dropped to almost a whisper as though she didn't want the others to hear. "Obviously you should tell Ms. Rhine," I said. "Don't you have security for this sort of thing?"

She shrugged again, her eyes avoiding mine. "They are looking into it."

She clearly wanted me to drop the subject so I let it go. We would be traveling together in the morning anyway, I thought. Maybe I could get her to open up about it on the flight.

As I was packing that night I called my friend Charles. The budget allowed me two assistants, not including the film crew who wouldn't be much help in any investigation. They'd just be in the way. Lewis had appointed his own protégé Mike as one of my two and I knew he'd be good for muscle but not much else. My own pick was Charles, my best friend since college and the only person I really trusted to have my back.

I called to tell him the job and what it paid. "You keep it," he said, referring to the money. "I'm in. You know I'm in."

I hadn't really questioned it. I didn't even try to get him to take the money. It was a pointless gesture and he would have been offended. Charles had briefly been a basketball star before he destroyed his knee. Now he made plenty from his retirement income and still did occasional endorsements so he had mostly free time and unlike me he didn't mind the attention from Lewis's show. I think he relished it.

Charles and I had met our first day at Blackstone, the social sciences college in Oklahoma where I studied media engagement theory and Charles was establishing competency in human history on a basketball scholarship. We hit it off immediately. I had seen him once before when I had come over the summer for scholarship testing. He had basketball camp at the same time and had already been getting a bit of a surprise buzz so it was hard not to notice him at the small school, the way he carried a charismatic sense of humor and a fairly sizable chip on the same shoulder.

We ended up rooming across from each other our introductory year. The first night we moved in, a week before classes, we stayed up all night talking – me, him, and his suite-mate Anton – until four in the morning, covering every topic from families, girlfriends, music and movies to philosophy, human versus alien consciousness, interstellar travel, and what it might be like to live on another planet. At that time only one of us had left Earth. Charles had played several games on Mars in high school but Mars then was just a human colony. What we all wanted was to visit an alien world.

Since then we both had plenty of chances and he, like me, embraced the opportunity for another. I agreed to pick him up in the morning.

It did not take me long to pack – I travel light and the wardrobe did most of the work – but like the night before I couldn't sleep thinking about the upcoming adventure. Eventually I got out of bed and spent another $40 for an hour on *Galactic Empires* where I modded gobo with the full sensory immersion.

Instead of jumping right into a game I first ran the "Introduction to Asitot" tutorial several times over. It wasn't that I needed the practice, I just wanted to take my time getting a feel for the world. They are never the same as Earth, you know. Asitot was inhabited mostly underground, which I initially thought would be claustrophobic but didn't seem that way at all in the game.

The third time I repeated the tutorial I discovered the instructor was not merely an AI when he said, "Greetings, sir. I had you on earlier. Are you struggling with anything in particular?" It still could have been an NP, of course, as that kind of friendly banter is standard coding but when I asked, "Are you an advanced help protocol?" he laughed and clarified:

"Oh, we are not bots, sir. I am proud to represent Asitot as part of our cultural outreach program. The first tutorial is automated but after that one of our representatives steps in to observe. It is our job to make sure you get the help you need. If I may ask sir, which game would you like to try?"

"Wait," I said. "You're from Asitot?" His appearance in the simulator was fully human.

"I am.

"A gobo?" I said.

"I am guvian, yes. I can switch to a guvian mod if that is more to your comfort." As it was he was a tall human man with a short beard and glasses while I was a short gobo, bald, squinting in the bright light.

"No," I said. "Human is fine."

"You are struggling with the eyes?" he asked. "Most players who repeat this zone say they are having trouble acclimating themselves to the *shatia*, which is what we call the membranes that cover the eyes. Remember it is not necessary to blink and when you do the *shatia* chosen will be dependent upon the pressure."

I had already mastered it, sort of. Though I had noticed if I didn't choose the same filters – the same *shatia* – every time it took a little while to figure out the order. Operating the mod hadn't been a problem for me. Still I blinked a few times as a little more practice never hurt anybody. There was no physical sensation other than the normal feeling of blinking, just the shifting in exposure and hue that came with the change of *shatia*. With one of the filters I could see prisms of light reflecting from the instructor's glasses but as the overall effect was far too bright in this environment I quickly shifted to another. "I have a question," I said. "How close would you say this is to the real experience?" I knew what seemed bright to me with these eyes wouldn't to my own. The caves of Asitot are dimmer than Earth's daylight by far so guvian eyes are accordingly more sensitive.

"It's difficult for me to say," said the trainer. "As I am guvian I cannot know how these scenes are perceived by one who is human."

"I guess I'm curious as to what I'm missing," I said.

"As I too am curious. I am told that humans envision with particular clarity. Or perhaps the word is consistency." He paused for a moment. "My translator recommends the words 'exactness.'"

"You speak anglish incredibly well," I said.

"Thank you. I have studied with fascination since childhood when I first saw the great cinematic *Mickey the Mouse*." He laughed. "I was very naïve. I believed truly that a mouse could grow over a meter tall." He paused a moment then politely asked, "Were you planning on playing a particular game?"

I hadn't really decided yet as my real interest had just been to acclimate myself to the environment. "That's what I was trying to figure out," I said. "I would like something immersive, culturally immersive. I'm more interested in a learning experience I suppose than strictly gaming."

"I understand, sir, and think it an excellent idea. Cultural exchange is one of the greatest benefits of the Galactic Empires gaming system. For the most realistic historical immersion I highly recommend the Ghaman Tournament. It is our version of your Kingdoms. You can even port a higher level character directly if you have one."

"I do." I didn't play Kingdoms much but I had worked my way up to mayor of a small city-state in Ancient Greece. I daydreamed briefly about what a level nine with that kind of influence would get me in the Ghaman Tournament but no doubt it would take all night just to convert my history unless I let the AI do it, which was not my style. It sounded interesting and educational, but... "I'm less interested in the historical side," I said. "What have you got that's more of an immediate experience? More recent, up to date?" I threw out Vavaka's home city. "I'd love to play something in Jebala. I'll be visiting soon."

"I see!" he said. "Very nice!" He seemed genuinely enthused. "With an entry-level character there are many options to explore. We have a game called Market Performer which you might enjoy if you are artistically inclined. Or if you are interested in the seedier side there is a criminal organization simulation called Masters of the Underworld. These are of course translations and both games offer a fully anglish immersive experience within Jebala."

I felt like I had wasted enough of his time so I thanked him and tried Market Performer as he had recommended. I spent a little extra time on the character creation section (since I went ahead and purchased a character instead of playing one of the temporary presets) and eventually came up with a gobo of Hullen descent — a nationality I had never heard of but which seemed vaguely similar to what we would call gypsies back on Earth. When the game began I was essentially a street beggar. I had chosen art instead of music, which meant I began with a pad of paper and a charcoal-like piece of rock — a fascinating thing, by the way, that was mostly dark purple but allowed for an incredible variety of shading and texture — plus the clothes on my back, no shoes included. For a half hour I stopped random strangers in the street and pressured them to pose for quick portraits. At the end of that time I had collected enough to buy a strange black drink that dubiously translated as "coffee" or an additional drawing rock of another color. I went with a second color, adding a versatile red. All that was secondary to my real intent to familiarize myself with the planet a little bit.

If you've played *Empires* you know the experience isn't quite perfect even in immersion mode. Nowadays it only seems to break apart a bit on the edges of your peripheral vision, but that minor static does serve as a small but constant reminder that it was all just a simulation. I assumed many if not most of the gobos I interacted with were NPC's. With a couple of my "customers" their behavior was shallow enough to make it obvious, but despite my minor complaints about the depth of the immersion it was real enough for my purposes.

I know that to human vision Asitot is dark like a late evening on Earth, lit mostly by bioluminescence and only recently electrics. Hence gobo eyes are incredibly sensitive, and I had no trouble seeing through any of my four *shatia* (I had hoped for more, but that aspect of character creation was randomized and I had my typical luck). The "market" I "performed" in existed inside a single enclave next to which ran a tunnel that served as road. Inside the enclave – which was as large as a football field – crevices had been carved, descending into the ground, and recessed into these were small shops and ad-hoc storefronts, with storage apparently kept underneath. I was pushed out of a few of these trenches by aggressive shopkeepers who tried to keep the space limited to customers, but I eventually found a place next to a friendly, chubby gobo selling candy treats to passing children.

He was playing a game called Solar Sweets, a small mod of Merchant Wars localized to Jebala. The gameplay was not too different from Market Performer and we occasionally were able to score off the same customers.

His name was Boodle, probably just a handle, and I stayed near him because he was naturally chatty and didn't hesitate to answer any of my random oddball questions. I told him I was human right from the start and he immediately broke into a smile.

"Ah, earthen are you? *Plasma Gate,* yes? Horaflik Fryday?"

Plasma Gate was a recent blockbuster movie – clearly a hit on Asitot – and Horaflik Fryday its main character, some sort of time-traveling hero, I thought, though I hadn't seen it myself. I couldn't remember the name of the actor who played the main character but I had never liked him – he had a monotone voice that sounded like he was reading and even when he did body work it always seemed stiff and uncomfortable. Anyway, out of respect for social niceties I didn't say so; instead I nodded knowingly as Boodle talked about his favorite scenes. I pretended it all made sense but it sounded like surreal pseudo-punk and his descriptions did not inspire me to go see it.

Eventually I was able to ask probing questions about what I was really interested in: guvian culture. What was it like to live on Asitot? He seemed to know Earth pretty well – he was a big fan of Hollywood and thought it would be amazing to see such a vivid sky, he said – but I had no such advantage. Guvian film was too visually complex for most humans and was not centered around plot like ours but instead around subtle visual symbolism developed from their own historical mores.

"I can't tell you much," he told me, "only what I've experienced myself." He blinked to a different *shatia* and looked me over. "You're Hullen, I take it, from your hair and your accent." I hadn't realized I had an accent – which of course was simulated since I was still speaking in my natural anglish – but as for hair I had almost none, just a very short layer of black fur on top of the head. Boodle on the other hand had longer locks, dark blue, styled into curls around his ears.

"Hullen, yes," I said. "I don't know much about it."

"Well," he said, "you're liable to get passed over by some. It's not that Hullen are disliked, you see? Just that a few of the tribes sort of pretend they don't exist."

Here the sim poked into the game – as discreetly as

28

possible – to offer alternative translations for the word "tribes:" "families," "races" and "religions" all popped up. This would only happen if the program considered the original guvian word to have no real anglish equivalent, so any attempt to make sense of it could be doomed to failure.

I mentioned it to Boodle and asked for clarification.

He took a moment, interrupted by a similar translation glitch, then said, "Religion?"

"Religion?" I repeated.

His brow cleared and he smiled. "Yes, religion. I use here the word 'religion,' which could also be for my tastes 'fantasy,' 'dream,' and 'conviction.' This is what you mean?"

I hesitated. "Well, what about culturally? What about beliefs? What, for instance, do the Hullen believe?"

"Beliefs?" he said. "You mean by this 'convictions,' 'knowledge,' or 'frame-of-reference?'"

Again the AI popped in to let me know that "frame-of-reference" was only a loose equivalency for the untranslatable *alojago*, which could perhaps also have meant "perspective," "alone-ness," or even "intense love or hatred."

I laughed and shrugged. Even with modern translation AI talking across interstellar cultures and languages was incredibly difficult. I thought of India Phoenix and wondered what kinds of conversations she had engaged in with her alien fiancé. I doubted India spoke guvian; did Vavaka know any anglish? Or would they be using a translator-bot on their honeymoon? "Alojago," I replied. "Tell me about that."

He interrupted me for a moment to haggle with a

young gobo child over the price of a long curly candy stick with a glob of goo at the end. The customer was likely an adult modding as a child judging by the way she tried to over-emphasize her cuteness, and Boodle wasn't fooled and gave her no discount.

"Now, you're Hullen," he said when he finished the transaction. "Being Hullen, you don't seem that weird when you watch over my shoulder like that because the Hullen, they don't care about proper behavior. Still, some types might really rough you up over it since Hullen aren't generally liked when they are noticed. Hullen go back a long ways digging where they shouldn't. But I guess most of us – I'm a Terwik you see – most of us are more scared of Hullen than anything else. They can go wild, you see? They break through walls on you that you didn't even know were there."

"I really didn't know which one to choose."

"Ha!" he said. "Well I'm a Terwik through and through, I wouldn't mod any other way. We all tend to think our own is best, right?" He sold a flimsy sheet of gel to a teenager, a shy sort that seemed a little lost. I sketched a quick profile of the same teen and pressured him into paying me too much for it. I suspect in reality it was a much younger kid underneath and I felt a mild guilt for powning the poor child, but it was a game, after all, and if you didn't want to get beat you shouldn't play it. I thought about what he had said, though, that we all thought our own was best, and I challenged him on it after we finished our transactions.

"I'm a human," I said, and he nodded – that was territory we'd already covered – "but I don't think humans are the best form of life out there. Do gobos think that?"

"Best of the gobonoids," he said, with a wry tone that I took to mean he was joking. He touched me on the shoulder in a friendly way. "We're all different. My family and Terwiks in general I think don't see much difference between the earthens and the Terwiks. But not all our kind feel that way. On Barnaby they like earthens so good they try to make Earth again out on the moon, but on Barnaby they have sky, you see? Like earthens have the sky. We gobos don't have any sky, but I have seen it in your movies, the stars you dream on. You are a funny Earthen modded Hullen. Hullens are suspicious of earthens, I think. Hullens don't know what to do with a sky, either. But who aren't the Hullen suspicious of? They know *every* kind going to take from the Hullen. You don't act much like a Hullen, so I knew you weren't gobo right away."

"You're perceptive," I said.

"It's true," he agreed modestly. "Probably most wouldn't notice a thing."

I nodded, thinking again of India, her distracted eyes always looking inward at herself, wondering if she had sensed anything odd about Vavaka that first meeting. What sort of human had he modded? What background? What nationality? What had she seen when she looked at whatever inane details he had no doubt randomly chosen? Or had he chosen them with more care? Was Vavaka, inter-galactic corporate giant, as naïve as India Phoenix, Earth-renowned celebrity socialite and heiress?

I was very curious to meet him.

I almost asked Boodle about Vavaka — he had surely

31

heard of him one would think — but I stopped myself at the last second, not sure what impulse caused my restraint. Boodle was friendlier than I could have hoped for (he encouraged me to friend his cell when I arrived on Asitot) but I had just come looking for cultural background, and he had certainly given me that.

What I had learned is that I knew next to nothing about guvian culture. But that was to be expected. Worlds were rich and deep. I thanked Boodle, exited the game after reaching level 3, and promised myself that I would tread lightly on Asitot. I had no reason to stir up any trouble on another planet. There was no reason to begin with any particular suspicions. Both Vavaka and India were important public figures and while I had a nice opportunity in this job to explore a new world, I had to do so quietly, in a way that stirred up no trouble for either of them. I would operate quietly and under the radar. As under the radar as possible, at least, with a 3V crew broadcasting every move.

I was able to sleep, finally, but my dreams were so full of my anticipations of Asitot that I might as well have kept playing *Galactic Empires*. I couldn't remember many details in the morning — I never could — but I remember that India Phoenix was featured heavily and I don't think she was human. But she wasn't gobo either, which was weird. I'm not sure what she was.

I thought about it as I flew to pick up Charles the next morning. In the dream, and in my mind later, it was more than just an idle detail. As far as I could recall, she had looked no different in the dream than in real life. I wasn't sure what made me think she had been anything other than her normal self, there had just been something different, something a little off. The dream had taken place in Jebala, I think, as I had a vague memory of the caves, the soft rainbows of ambient lighting. Maybe I had thought her a gobo or something similar, a passing fancy, but I didn't think that was it. I mentioned the dream to Charles as he was directing his luggage into the bay.

"So you're hot for India Phoenix, what of it? Most of the planet is."

"I didn't say I was hot for her," I protested.

"Well I don't know what other meaning you're looking for. You met India Phoenix — who is fine as a fox by the way — and you dreamed about getting down all night. Nothing to be ashamed of."

"That's not what happened," I said. But my protest sounded feeble even to myself.

"It's just a dream," he said. "Quit complaining. I barely got any sleep at all. I was up all night researching."

"Interstellar or WWW?"

"A bit of both. Worldwide doesn't have enough details about the other planets if you ask me. It's mostly fake v-scenes and fan-feeds that might as well be promos."

"You have to stick with the pedias," I said.

"Too vague."

"So what did you find on the ISR?"

"You name it," he said. "I got heavily embroiled in the politics. Listen — they are not like us."

I didn't remind him aliens never were. I had figured

Charles would dive into the political side, it was why I myself hadn't bothered. We hopped aboard a shuttle to the Space Machine and on the way I asked him to fill me in on the details. He sighed heavily and shook his head.

"Too much, too much," he said. "But let me start with some history."

So he did, a narrative that continued sporadically throughout the morning. No one was sure where gobos had originated on the planet. There were three ancient civilizations that most of their modern ideas could be traced to. Jebala was a part of the North, which had before the appearance of civilization been a kingdom slowly growing over a thousand years. It had been built essentially on a hereditary monarchy, but, like with Earth, civilization had changed all that and replaced it with an Arbiter. Monarchies were viewed by Civilization as a transitional cultural adaptation to be replaced upon reaching cultural maturity. This change was often met with some resistance, but it never lasted long with the weight of Interplanetary Civilization behind the new order. Charles tried to explain how the North had managed the replacement of such an old system but it was complex and none of us followed. A caste system of some sort had been in place, no doubt well understood by the Northerners, but whatever unwritten rules had guided it were incomprehensible to an outsider. Charles admitted he hadn't truly been able to make sense of it himself.

We joined India at the Space Machine gate, along with her small entourage that she quietly encouraged to wait in a distant sitting area. I told Lewis's 3V crew to join them and we were blessed with the opportunity for some privacy — though it didn't save us from Mike, Lewis's assistant, who saw himself as one of us.

He argued with Charles here and there through his historical discourse — it was Mike's way — but India was all ears, as though the information was new to her. It was, I suspected, as she hadn't before seemed even to know the difference between Barnaby and Asitot. Which, as Charles explained, was a significant one. Philosophically they were diametrically opposed, with Barnaby embracing a connection to the outside universe while Asitot still seemed to resent the intrusion.

We had to wait for about an hour and a half while the Space Machine cycled through the star series. It was enough time for the four of us to get comfortable with each other. Charles had an easy time with India, but of course he was no stranger to celebrity. Mike had his usual awkward way about him, and I sat mostly silent, listening, thinking about the day ahead.

Finally we were ushered in to where we could see the Space Machine and all conversation ceased. I had been there before — we all had — but even so, when you first came around the corner and caught sight of it through the giant window it took your breath away. It was impossible to tell its size. At the moment it turned slowly, the bright lights seeming to arc in a kaleidoscopic display. Once we were inside it would turn so fast it would seem to become a single disc of light.

"Amazing," said Mike.

"It is," I said. "You have mustard on the side of your

mouth." I couldn't help grinning in anticipation as I stepped up to the desk.

"All food and drink must be disposed of before entering the gate," the robot said as she handed us our pills. "All earthens are required to take the minimum dosage for your own safety."

I swallowed the little green capsule. The others did the same. The effects hit me immediately and I giggled.

"Fun," I said. "Fun flight."

India's smile looked the way mine felt. "Yeah," she said. "So fun."

And it was. Things didn't get ugly until we arrived on the other side and hopped on our shuttle to Asitot.

••••3••••

BUT DON'T LET ME GET AHEAD OF MYSELF. You may have never taken a journey on the Space Machine or even flown a shuttle to its gates (and why would you if you weren't going to ride the Machine itself?), in which case you might be unfamiliar with the procedure. We took the pills as required, then wandered down the long hallway to the pods. The hallway was about half the width of a football field and hundreds of people – human and otherwise – walked the same direction we did until we were finally filtered numerically into smaller sections. Each traveler had a pre-assigned pod, loosely configured for the comfort of each particular species. For humanoids it was a soft bed with soft walls and even a soft ceiling. The effect of the pill was such that it was easy to imagine one was floating in a giant marshmallow.

We said "Good flight" to each other and settled in, and within a few minutes I was sleeping. At least it felt like sleep, but I feel like a fragment of a memory of the transition remains. Did I dream it? Or do I remember it somehow from an unconscious experience? Who can say? But my dreamlike memory of the moment when we disappeared in one portion of the universe and instantly reappeared in another is one of profound loss and profound gain at the same time. I remember thinking about how much one could experience in the quiet dark with only the soft sensation of the pillows surrounding, how much of life could be squeezed into such a small space and a tiny moment. So I must have been at least a little awake.

A gentle tone sounded after the transition, waking me from my trance-like state, and my little door slid silently open. I stepped out and joined the others in the hall. We followed the crowd out the gate then separated, as Vavaka's shuttle was held separately in a private garage. As we walked there I overheard Charles ask India how she enjoyed the transition.

"Oh, it's not my first time," she said. "But it was fun." She had traveled many times even as a child and just recently shot a movie on location in the Artemis system. Maybe she was more familiar with the outside universe than I had given her credit for.

By now the effects of the drug had worn off, even though very little time had actually passed. The transition itself was instantaneous, but it caused the body to experience time differently. Despite what might have been only five or ten minutes of actual sleep we all felt very refreshed. At least I did, and from the spring in their step it looked like the others did too.

We were at Pyramus. It didn't feel different yet, but we still hadn't left the station. We exited with the same crowd we had entered, mostly humans, a good proportion of gobos, and a scattered selection of other humanoids. Our group split off and made our way to the back. We were met by a gobo who spoke excellent anglish. He was about my height — which is short for a human, even shorter for a gobo — but stockier with a wide face and a welcoming smile that seemed almost human.

"You are with Vavaka?" he said to India. "I recognize you from the tube."

"The tube," India laughed. "How funny!"

He looked embarrassed, his smile sagging. "I am so very sorry. I have been misunderstood?"

"Not at all," I said. "It's just one doesn't hear 3V called that much anymore."

"3V is earthen vid, yes?" he said. "Yes, earthen vid is tube. It is what you call slang, yes? Or low down? I hope I don't offend. My son uses these words, but I myself know almost no low down."

I told him I didn't either, and introduced myself. Mike and Charles did the same, while the 3V crew — which consisted of two cameraman and a pair of angry looking women which I believed to be the director and her assistant — silently captured every frame. The two bodyguards watched grimly from the side.

"Please follow me," the gobo said. "I am Wilam, your driver pilot. I will take you to Asitot."

He led us down the deck and into the shuttle tube. He told us about himself along the way. He himself did not know Vavaka but had been hired just to take us to Asitot and to serve as our guide and driver if needed once we arrived.

"Wonderful," said India, and seemed to really mean it, while her two bodyguards stepped forward to pat him down. Have I introduced the bodyguards? No? That's probably because they never introduced themselves. One was large and silent, the other was larger and more silent. I figured them to be a part India's regular entourage. They were human, both square-jawed and rectangular, both with dark hair cropped close to the head. The only things that separated them were a slight difference in height and the fact that one – the taller – wore a plastic tie while the other wore the open collar.

Both also wore opaque bi-cells – the phones that looked like wraparound sunglasses – and I assumed they, like the 3V crew, were recording everything.

Anyway, Wilam was exceptionally friendly and chatted amiably as he led us down the tube. He was a father of three, well-traveled, originally from Barnaby, Asitot's moon. We arrived shortly at a large first-class cabin, more spacious than I'd ever personally seen in a taxi shuttle.

"Adula and Ruisha will be happy to serve food and drinks once we are in transit," Wilam said as two guvian attendants appeared to prepare us for the flight. "Please get settled and we will take off as soon as you are ready."

Adula was a tall willowy female, Ruisha an equally tall, equally willowy male. They moved like graceful blades of grass swishing gently in the wind. Ruisha helped us each with our lap belts while Adula took drink orders. I requested a blue soviet, as did India – she said she'd never tried one – and both Charles and Mike had beers.

The larger of the guards stayed with us in the cabin,

as did both cameramen, hoping they said to capture some b-roll conversation. The director and the other guard disappeared into the back of the shuttle, while Wilam, Adula, and Ruisha left us to prepare for the flight.

"This is a U-Ship shuttle?" Charles asked. He looked to India for an answer but she gave him a blank expression and shrugged. "Must be," he answered himself. "Why would Vavaka use anything else?"

"It's a TR-1900. Earthen construction," said Mike.

"How do you know?" I asked him.

"I made a model once," he said. "Do you play Space Racer? I'm a level nineteen."

"I don't," I said. "Is this a racer?"

"No," he said, "but you can make all types. Maybe he uses TR-1900s for U-Ship."

"Maybe it's a rental," I said. "It could belong to Wilam."

I felt a mild vibration as we took off, well insulated by the fine construction of the ship. The shuttle moved so smoothly and effortlessly we might still have been sitting in the hangar. "Windows please," said India, and the walls of the cabin became transparent. We watched the hangar slowly shrink into the distance behind us.

Ahead, Asitot was still just the tiniest dot in the sky, pale yellow against the black. I could barely keep my eyes off it as it grew ever so slowly to where I could just start to see a hint of texture, the atmosphere that covered the surface. Asitot was a desert planet, more common as far as nucleic life was concerned than our own watery variety. Continents as we understood them were not a thing on Asitot. Instead there were only a few lakes scattered across the planet and gobos throughout their history had commonly lived underground. Some activity happened on the surface, especially during the long hours of dusk and dawn, but most of the habitation took advantage of the cool temperatures below the surface where underground reservoirs of water supported a population only about one fifth of Earth's thirty billion.

I had read up as much as I could on the planet, but I still had no idea what to expect other than what little I had been able to glean from playing in the simulated environment and watching clips on 3V. It had a geography, despite its desert nature, as rich and as varied as Earth, and a history equally so. I had no context, no connection with the planet on which to build an expectation.

While I stared, transfixed, the others talked about games – a common topic – and I tuned out until Ruisha brought me my soviet. "Your drink, sir. You are welcome at this point to move about the cabin."

I thanked him and stood up to stretch my legs as he and Adula disappeared into the connecting service compartment. The blue soviet was a little dry, exactly the way I preferred it.

"How long is the flight?" Charles asked.

"Two more hours," said Mike. "But you know they don't count hours on Asitot, they do it in quarter-turns. They keep time completely different here."

"What's a quarter-turn?" asked India.

"That's a translation. They've got their own name for it," Mike said. "I don't remember what that is. But it's like a fourth a day, you know, when the planet rotates?

42

You divide it four times. It takes like seventy hours you know. It's real slow."

I happened to be the only one looking out the window at this point so I was the first to see the ship approaching us from behind. It was much larger than ours — clearly not a taxi shuttle — and moving much faster. At first I thought it was about to pass but then it turned more deliberately in our direction.

"Charles," I interrupted, "what do you make of that?" He looked over my shoulder. There was a moment of silence as we all looked at the window screen.

"Definitely an Asitot ship," he said. "Guvian."

"Yeah, we don't build them in levels like that," I agreed. Whereas earthen space ships were sleek aerodynamic looking affairs developed from the lineage of the airplane, gobos designed theirs more like dwellings, larger metal versions of their traditional housing. The craft we were looking at was stacked four cubes high, lined with an impressive array of weaponry.

"I think that's a battleship," said Mike, sounding surprised. "I mean it has to be. It's a class 4 at least, and what else would that be?"

At that point the bodyguard who had stayed in the cabin came over to take a look. "Move," he said roughly to Mike, who shifted over immediately. The guard scowled at the window, his fingers madly pressing buttons on the side of his bi-cell.

India put a hand on his thick bicep. "Nikolo, what's going on?"

He ignored her and spoke instead to his cell: "Of course, sir. Immediately." He turned away from the window and grabbed India by the arm. "Miss Phoenix, please come with me. Everyone else remain still. No one move."

"What's going on?" demanded Mike.

Nikolo gave him an angry look. "Until I know that none of you can be trusted. Miss Phoenix, please accompany me to the security cabin."

The door slid open and he dragged her through it. The window display remained active, and we watched the Guvian ship approach. Just the five of us were left in the cabin — Mike, Charles, myself and the two cameramen. We waited, but no one returned to tell us what was going on.

• • • • 4 • • • •

CHARLES WAS FIRST TO BREAK THE SILENCE. "I'm not waiting," he said. "I'm going to find out what's up."

He stepped toward the door but it didn't automatically open as it should have. Instead the light above turned red – meaning the door had been secured. Charles waved his hand over the sensor then pressed the manual emergency button repeatedly to no effect.

"They've got us trapped in here," said Mike, his fat forehead sliced with worry.

"Try the others," Charles said, by which he meant the two other doors, the aft door leading back into the coach area, the other the starboard door to the service compartment that kept Adula and Ruisha. There were no other exits from the cabin. The door Charles had tried – the one Nikolo and India had disappeared through – was the forward door that led in the direction of the pilot. One of the cameraman attempted to open the coach door and I tried the service compartment but both lit red and refused to open.

"I don't like this," said the other cameraman,

scratching furiously at his beard. "I'm calling the director." He wore a slim glasses-style dual cell. He touched the side, wiggled his fingers, then shook his head. "I'm not getting any service at all. I don't even have a local connection. We should at least be able to connect to our CAP." He was most likely referring the to the director's cell transmitter, which would have been acting as central access point for the whole video crew. My own cell was serving as CAP for the investigative crew of myself, Charles and Mike. My cell, a LashLens 4, showed no service, but I tried calling Charles using the CAP and his cell rang immediately, playing a quietly aggressive hop-core tune. He checked the ID, saw it was me, and gave me a puzzled look.

"Just checking our own service," I explained. "I don't have any outside connection either, but local access seems fine." I turned back to the bearded cameraman, who seemed to be the senior of the two. I was pretty sure I had met him before on another shoot for Lewis but I couldn't remember his name, just that it started with a J. John, Jack, Jerry, something like that. "Any reason your director would have turned her phone off?"

John Jack or Jerry raised his eyebrows and shook his head in the negative. "When she went back there she told us to call if we needed her." He seemed angry about this, as though that minor decision of the director's had led to our current predicament. He turned to the other cameraman. "What do you think, Jack?" This was apparently the name of the other cameraman so I decided for no particularly good reason the first must be Jerry.

Jack shook his head, indicating he had no thoughts on the matter.

"There's a service com," Mike said, pointing to a small unobtrusive switch and speaker panel by the service door. He flipped it on. "Hello?" he said. We waited but there was no response.

"I don't like this at all," said Charles. He crossed the cabin and moved Mike aside, then knocked several times on the service compartment door. It was solid metal like the others and probably soundproof but he put his ear up against it anyway. Then he pounded even harder. "They've got to be on the other side," he said. "There's no other way through the ship."

"You mean the attendants?" said Mike.

"Of course the attendants," said Charles. "Adula and the other one, the dude." He moved next to the coach door and repeated the knocking-listening-pounding procedure with the same result. The definition of madness, I thought about telling him.

The window screen was still functioning, but most of the approaching ship was no longer in view. From what I could tell both ships had come to a complete stop. This combined with our proximity led me to conclude we were being boarded.

Charles gave up on the doors and joined me in my bleak survey of our situation. I could tell by the movement of thoughts over his face as he came to the same conclusion I had.

"Pirates," he said grimly.

"Impossible," said Jerry. "Not this close to Asitot."

"You wouldn't think so," said Mike, his voice high-pitched when he was anxious. "This is a Civilization system with a B+ travel grade."

"Maybe we're just getting pulled over," said Jack.

"That doesn't look much like a Civilization ship to me," said Charles. "Of course I'm not from the area. Maybe the local ones are different."

"A Civilization ship that size would be properly marked," I said. "It would be uncivilized not to identify your purpose. I'm afraid Charles is right. I think we're being attacked by pirates."

"Why won't someone tell us what's going on?" demanded Mike, flipping the com switch back and forth. "Miss Phoenix? Mr. Wilam? Anyone?"

"Turn it off," Charles growled at him. "You want to lead them right to us?"

"If it is pirates this is where they'd come anyway, don't you think?" I asked him. "You have to assume they're looking for India Phoenix. I seriously doubt this is a random attack. They must have known she was on board. Maybe it's a ransom?"

Jerry and Jack looked at each other. "Focus!" said Jerry. "You're responsible for catching this footage. I guess I'm acting director until we're back online with Gina." Jack snapped to attention, though he didn't look very happy about it. He pressed a button or two on his cell and waggled his fingers, typical behavior for someone working through the menus of a complicated app.

"I guess this is good entertainment," I said dryly.

"Gina would not be happy if we didn't get all the reaction shots," said Jerry. "Hey, I think it's ridiculous, we need to focus on our safety. But I'm on the job, you know? Twenty-four seven. I'm still paying off two divorce settlements, you believe it? I'm only thirty-five." He scratched at his beard again and I could tell he was nervous. He seemed the type to get worked up easily but I didn't remember him being so chatty. "I just need to keep this job," he said. "I've got two strikes already."

"I'm sorry," Jack interrupted, touching Charles gently on the shoulder. A dangerous move, and he pulled back when Charles scowled at him. "I'm very sorry," he said again. "Can I just get you to pound on the service door again? I'd like to get a slightly more dramatic framing."

"Are you kidding me?" Charles demanded.

"Well, we couldn't really see your face," Jack said.

"Charles, it would be helpful," I said. "Lewis will definitely want that shot in the show."

Charles looked at me like he couldn't decide if I was serious or making fun of him. Finally he sighed and said, "Fine, whatever." He moved back to the service door, knocked, listened, pounded. He went with it too, really overdoing the facial expressions, knotting his brow, clenching his jaw when his ear was pressed to the door so you could see the vein pop out in his temple. "That better?" he asked. "Or do you need another take."

"Perfect," said Jack. "Really good." He looked at Jerry for approval, who nodded. "Do you mind doing one more?" Jack asked.

"I think that's enough," I said. I was trying not to show it but I too was aggravated and – to be honest – scared. Maybe it wasn't pirates out there, but what seemed to me the most logical explanation was that someone – be it pirates, mercenaries, whatever – was trying to kidnap India for ransom. Where did that leave us? Criminals that would be so bold this close to Asitot would no doubt be ruthless as well. Surely they had a lot to gain – the Phoenix family was plenty rich – but our shuttle was on a schedule. If we were delayed very long it would attract notice. How long had we been stopped already?

We were trapped meanwhile in a closed space, access to which was controlled from the outside. My eyes and thoughts landed on the red security light above the door to the pilot's cabin.

"We need to secure these doors," I said. Charles frowned, thinking it over. Jack did a weird sidestep as he moved to zoom in on my face.

"What are you talking about?" Mike asked. "They're already secured." All heads turned to look at the various doors, each showing the same red light.

"I don't mean through their system." As I talked I climbed up onto a cabinet by the service compartment door, a sturdy wooden piece firmly affixed to the wall. "If they really have taken us hostage who do you think has access to these doors? Wilam?" I stretched as high as I could and peered closely at the wall next to the security light where I could make out the thin creases of an inset panel. "I need something thin," I said. "Something to pry out this panel." As Charles and Mike began searching the room I pushed against the panel and felt it give ever so slightly. "Wait, maybe I can break it." I hit it with my fist a couple times, causing a slight dent to appear, but it didn't give.

"Hold on," said Charles, "I have a laser app on my cell. Switch places with me."

I stepped down and he climbed up onto the cabinet,

his titanium knee making a dull thud as he used it to brace himself. He was about fifteen centimeters taller than me and twenty-five kilograms more massive, so he didn't get up there as easily, but once he was standing he was eye-level with the panel so his cell was only centimeters from it. He pushed against it as I had, then waved his fingers in the air, app-menu style. A thin beam of red light appeared from his cell, creating a slight trail of smoke where it seared the panel. Charles moved his head with care, cutting carefully around the edges. He cut about halfway, enough that he could bend the panel out and expose the circuitry behind it.

"I don't really know what I'm looking at," he said. "You can hack it to open the door?" The others all exchanged looks at the word hacking, as even suggesting it was probably uncivilized.

"There's no way you can hack it without a terminal," I said. "I'm just hoping we can disable it. I doubt that will open the door but it may keep our attackers from opening it either."

He gave me a skeptical look. "You're not going to get us trapped in here permanently, are you?"

I shook my head like the idea was ridiculous. "We'd have to disable all of the doors for that to even be remotely possible. Trade me places again."

He climbed down and I climbed up. I didn't know much about what I was seeing but at least it was earthen. Behind the panel was a blue circuit board, larger than the panel, so that I couldn't see the edges. Two spots glowed with dark green light and beneath these was a small crevice that I recognized as a QOI port. So I *could* maybe hack it using my cell but since I was hardly an expert on door security I didn't risk it.

Above the green spots was a small white circle and this looked more like what I needed. I couldn't be sure but I suspected this was the relay nexus — basically where the processor from the door connected to the main computer.

"Hand me your cell," I said to Charles. "Or can you zap me that laser app on the local network?"

"Hold on," he said. He waggled his finger and a moment later I received a notification — "YOU HAVE RECEIVED AN APP FROM CHARLES THOMAS. INSTALL?"

I said yes and clicked through several warnings about the app's age rating, safety rating, and legal usage. It wasn't legal, either on Earth or on a transport shuttle, which was probably why I didn't already have it installed. I wondered how he had acquired it and how much it had cost him.

"You're going to get me in trouble," I said, but he just shrugged. It didn't look like the idea bothered him.

The app had a targeting system, which was nice, and I calibrated it to my vision, focused my eye on the relay nexus, and turned the laser on. It was set to a low intensity by default so I raised it until I could see the nexus start to smoke and smell it burning. A second later it popped, causing us all to jump and me to nearly fall off the cabinet.

Luckily the laser app had a safety feature that turned it off immediately when it sensed sudden movement.

"It looks like it worked," Charles said. He pointed above the door where the red light had turned black.

"But it didn't open the door," Mike said.

"That's what I expected," I said. "That door was just a

test."

"You've trapped the stewards," he objected.

"Possibly," I said. "But unless pirates somehow got through to that compartment at least they're entirely safe until we figure this out."

"I don't like this," said Jack, but Jerry waved him to silence.

"Now what?" asked Charles. "Cockpit?"

I took a second to think it through. The window feed, uninterrupted, showed the attacking ship behind us in the direction of the coach cabins. This was also the direction Nikolo had taken India, to the security cabin, he had said, no doubt to meet up with the rest of the security team.

If the pirates knew what they were doing — and I was assuming they did as they clearly knew we were carrying an expensive celebrity — they probably had anticipated this move.

"How could they have entered the ship?" I asked this question aloud but no one answered. I didn't expect anyone to. I continued. "The only entrance to the shuttle is from the front, correct? Did they park behind us and make their way around? I doubt it. Don't we have to assume they've somehow cut their way into the cabin behind?"

"We don't know for sure anyone's entered the ship at all," said Mike. "I should try the com again."

"Don't touch that switch," Charles said.

It would only take three or four prepared assailants to overcome the security guards, I thought. "What will they do when they've acquired their target?" I continued my internal monologue aloud. "How have they disabled the pilot?"

"We need to get control of the ship," Charles said. "If they came in through the back they've already got India or they'd be retreating."

It was the same conclusion I had come to. "I will disable the door to the back," I said. "We can't count on security to come save us. If anybody comes through there they are probably not our friends." I climbed up to look for the panel above the coach door. It took me a few seconds to find it but once I did I was able to cut through and disable it quickly, preparing myself for the explosive pop this time so I didn't nearly kill myself.

"We still need to get through this door," said Charles, putting his hands against the surface of our only way through to the cockpit.

"What about the pilot?" said Mike. "Why hasn't he come back here?"

"Hard to say," I said. "But it was probably Wilam who disabled the doors. I could be wrong. I don't know enough about these shuttles to know whether that would be done by the pilot or from the security cabin."

"You think he's part of this?" Charles asked.

"The pilot?" Charles nodded, and I shrugged. "Why did he stop? He could have received any kind of communication or threat that we don't know about." I turned to Mike. "Now that we've gotten our backs secured go ahead and turn that com on."

Mike frowned but flipped the switch as I had asked him to.

"Close-up on the switch," whispered Jerry urgently to Jack, who looked hassled and swung around for a new angle.

I stepped up to the com speaker, deliberately forcing Jack to have to adjust. Not very nice of me, I know. "Wilam," I said into the com, "if you can hear me please respond."

I waited but there was no immediate reply. I exchanged looks with Charles, then repeated the request. A second later another voice — decidedly not Wilam's — came through.

"I am speaking to Mr. Gregory?" The voice was chilling; cold, precise, speaking anglish like a native.

"I'm Mr. Gregory," I confirmed. But I didn't like how this had turned at all. Of course they — whoever they were — would have information on us, I had already realized that. But this gobo calling me by my name gave it a decidedly personal feeling.

"I am looking forward to meeting you," the voice said and the knot in my stomach tightened. "I see you have disabled the access door. Futile. We could simply cut through to your compartment if we wished."

I wasn't the only tense one. Everyone in the room had frozen in place, eyes wide, listening intently.

"Then why don't you?" I demanded.

"I have what I desire," he said. "Later, I will acquire all the pieces I need."

"Who are you? What's your name?"

"What are names?" he shot back, and I realized with sudden clarity I was talking to a madman. This was no pirate, or, as I had also considered, some political game... Now I heard in his tone a psychotic element that meant we were in even greater danger. "What of your name?" he went on. "I have another for you. 309J236. Sound familiar?"

"Sounds as familiar as any other random string of numbers," I said. It meant nothing to me. "What have you done with India and Wilam?"

Charles and Mike were both staring at me intently and Jack moved to get a better shot of my face. I felt like an intense burden had suddenly been placed on my shoulders.

"They are both fine," said the voice, then added as though an afterthought: "Though their bodies are mere constructs, so what does it matter? You want that I should worry about that which is temporary, a fleeting illusion at most? No, 309. Hardly so."

I resisted the temptation to ask what the number meant. "It sounds like you are worried about it," I said. "I can hear it in your voice."

"Stay out," he said coldly. I had no idea what he meant. "India is mine. She will tell you so."

"India?" I asked urgently. "You have her there?"

"Not yet," he said. "She will tell you later. Now, 309J, you will listen."

I interrupted, since I hated that sort of power-grabbing demand. "I don't think I will." I stepped over to the com, my attitude rather childish, really, and flipped the com off.

I expected someone to object, but instead Charles handed me a napkin from the seat and gestured toward my face. "Your nose is bleeding."

I wiped at it and discovered he was right. I sighed then flipped the com back on. "Are you still there?"

His voice came back immediately as though he had been waiting. "You are engaging, 309, or I would indulge myself in irritation. But I appreciate your thorny

56

nature, for we are one and the same, you and I."

"We are nothing alike," I said.

"Don't worry, I do not intend you any harm," he said. "My intentions for you are grander, 309, than you can yet comprehend. All is not quite in place yet or I would tell you more. We can hardly be complete, you see, until I myself am complete. And for that to happen India must be one of us. I don't expect you to understand at this moment, but you will."

"I doubt it," I said. "You're a madman."

There was a moment of silence. "I'm not at all mad," he said. "Never think that, three zero nine." He emphasized the numbers as though they were an insult, enunciating each as though it had special meaning.

"What are your intentions with India?" I said. "I assume you are interested in ransom. How can you guarantee her safety?"

The voice on the com laughed, a sound so devoid of humor that it made my skin crawl. "I don't have any interest in ransom. You can keep your money and you can tell the Phoenix family the same. If I wanted to take it, I could take it other ways."

"If you hurt her we'll come after you," Charles interjected. "You sound like you think you're invincible. I can show you different." I put a hand on his shoulder and shook my head. I didn't want him riling up our unpredictable lunatic. Charles gave me an irritated look but backed down.

"Is that Charles Thomas?" the voice asked. "Of course it is. I believe you will come after me, it's what you're made for. But you would whether I hurt her or not, so what difference does it make whether I do?"

"What are your demands?" I said.

"I have no demands. I am done here. Mr. Gregory, we will continue our discussion in the future. Tra la."

"What's your name?" I asked quickly, but there was no response. "Why have you done this?" But already I could see in the window display the kidnapper's ship moving, separating from our shuttle. Jerry, noticing the same thing, waved at Jack to get footage of its departure.

"He's leaving," Mike said, unnecessarily.

"We're on a station schedule," Charles said. "We're way behind. Give it long enough and they'll send a law-ship out after us."

"We could wait for that," I said. "But people could still be in danger. We have no idea what he's done to Wilam or the rest of the crew. Charles, how long do you think it would take you to cut through to the pilot?"

"You mean through the door?" He shrugged. "It's like three centimeters. Probably six or seven minutes."

"Meanwhile, I'll work on this one," I said, indicating the passage to the coach and security cabin.

"Set it at its highest," Charles said, "it'll cut through just about anything."

I cut a square about two thirds of a meter across, drawing the lines first then retracing over and over again as it gradually burned deeper and deeper through the metal. My back started to hurt with the repeated motion of stooping, crouching and standing. I looked over to Charles to see if he was having the same problem but he had chosen to cut in a circle, standing in one spot the whole time. It looked a little better, maybe, but it seemed like it was hell on the neck.

"It smells terrible," Mike said.

Not just that, a moment later a light sprinkle of water showered us when the fire alarms went off. This also caused the one door we hadn't disabled — the one Charles was working on — to open automatically. "Nice," Charles said.

"Go check on Wilam," I said. I waved at Jerry. "You go with him." I turned back to my own work, which had to be almost complete, I thought. I had burned through at least a couple centimeters. I focused on the task and a minute later I was able to push the square of metal through to the other side where it clattered loudly onto the floor of the passageway. The resulting hole was big enough I could easily squeeze my shoulders through and crawl to the other side, but Mike, who was much bigger than me, gave it a skeptical look.

"You don't have to come with," I said, shuffling through and looking back at him. "I'll be fine. The bad guys are already gone."

"I'm coming," he said, and backed through, feet first, pulling his arms last, so that it stretched his shirt up to his nipples. Not the approach I would have taken, as I think it even exaggerated his size. But eventually he joined me on the other side.

I looked back through the hole at Jack, lifting an eyebrow to ask if he was coming. He did, having no trouble at all as he was about my size. The passageway was narrow and more dimly lit than the cabin had been. Jack looked back at the light coming through the cutout and said, "How would you feel about going back through again. It would be a more dramatic angle if I could get it from this side."

"No," I said shortly. "It's a waste of time and besides I'm not going to put Mike through that."

"Thank you," said Mike. Jack looked disappointed.

"At least let me vid you from the front," he said, and moved ahead of us, walking backwards. "Don't look at me," he said – responding no doubt to my irritated scowl – "just pretend I'm not here."

"Fine," I said. "I won't even warn you if I see a pirate, a kidnapper, a booby trap, depressurized cabin, anything like that." I was joking, of course. We could easily see to the end of the passageway, the door to the coach cabin lit with a green light. Were the cabin depressurized it would have secured itself immediately. Not that there couldn't be a pirate or kidnapper still on the other side, but this too seemed unlikely.

I acted nonchalant, but to tell the truth I was terrified. I didn't expect any more overt danger, not right at the moment, but I feared what we would find on the other side of the door. At best the room was empty, but even then our situation had changed dramatically. What had been a simple inter-planetary investigation – practically a field trip – had turned into a kidnapping, a hostage situation, and a criminal conspiracy with who-knew-what sort of political and legal implications on Asitot.

I stopped Jack before he reached the door's sensor. "You two get behind me, just in case."

Mike gave me a stern look and put a fat paw on my shoulder. "I don't think so, Mr. Gregory. This is my job." He moved me behind him and activated the sensor. The door opened with a smooth swish and my eyes immediately fell on the two bodies in the corner.

"Oh my," said Jack. "It's Gina and Susan." He started

toward the two figures then drew back. "Do you think they're okay?"

I saw no sign of blood or injury but I didn't think they were okay. They looked like rag dolls, one thrown on top of the other. I recognized the director, Gina, buried beneath the other, her long black hair disappearing under one of the seats. The other woman had short red hair cropped close to the head. Her face was visible, turned directly towards us. Her eyes were closed. I guess she could have been sleeping but I doubted it.

"You want to go back and wait for us?" I asked Jack. "It's not a problem."

He took a few deep breaths and shook his head. "They're dead, aren't they?" He lifted his shoulders with effort and gave me a brave look. "No, I've got to get footage. Gina would want quality footage." He thought about it again, though, and his face crumbled. He looked at me for guidance. "Would she? Would she want footage?"

I sighed. "I don't know, Jack. I really couldn't say." I stepped up to the bodies, putting two fingers to Susan's neck to verify what I already knew. "No pulse," I said. "I'm sorry, Jack."

"How did they die?" asked Mike. "How did he do it?"

"I don't know," I said again. I checked Gina as well, trying to disturb the bodies as little as possible. Jack looked at me with a brief spark of hope but I shook my head.

There were two more doors leading out of the coach cabin. One I presumed to be security. The other I immediately realized connected to the same service cabin that Adula and Ruisha had disappeared into. I stepped first to the service door. It opened with a wave of my hand and fearing the worst I stepped through. Adula and Ruisha lay discarded in a corner, arranged in an eerily similar fashion to how we had found Gina and Susan.

There's no way to describe how I felt then. Hopeless, defeated. My stomach turning, but not in nausea or terror, just a cold, sinking feeling of loss. I didn't know any of these people well but to be a part of life turning so suddenly to death made me cold.

I closed the service door and moved to security. I took a deep breath and waved at the sensor. The door slid open and now — now I felt nauseous. Nikolo and his partner did not appear to be sleeping as the others had. They looked instead like they had been beaten, their faces bruised, bloody, practically unrecognizable. And they were clearly dead, each with a charred, black hole in the center of the forehead.

·····5·····

I CLOSED THE DOOR AND ALSO MY EYES, taking several deep breaths to steady myself. It took a few seconds before I could clear the image from my mind. Jack, meanwhile, had seen everything as he followed me to each door to get footage. He looked at me with wide, frightened eyes, his mouth slightly open, trembling from head to toe. Still he tried to do his job, manipulating his cell with a variety of focused gestures. Based on the complexity of the motions his camera app was not simple to operate, but professional quality stuff rarely was.

"What is it?" said Mike, who at first had been preoccupied with his inspection of Gina and Susan but now saw the expression on our faces. I don't know how I looked but Jack's face was pale and it seemed like he had aged ten years in five minutes. Mike shook his head grimly. "They're all dead, aren't they?"

"Yes," I said.

"How?" he said, his voice tinged with desperation as though our lives depended on the answer. "Some kind of poison?" He clutched at my arm. "How did he do it?"

I shook him off. I had no desire to revisit the details and didn't think a grisly description was warranted. Mike was just muscle. "I don't know, I told you. I think both security guards were shot with a laser. Assassinated, it looked like." Jack took a position where he could capture both of us in the image at the same time, in profile.

"Everyone's dead," said Mike.

"Well, we're not. Not yet," I said.

The door swooshed open and Charles came in followed by Jerry. Charles looked grim but I saw no sign of the same devastation I was feeling. "We found Wilam," he said. "He's unconscious but it doesn't look like he's been hurt. I think he's okay. It's hard to tell. He's been drugged or something." His eyes fell on the bodies in the corner. "Are they all right?"

"I'm afraid not," I said. "They're not breathing."

Charles being Charles had to check for himself. He gave me a long, tired look and shook his head. I waved him over to the security door and allowed him a quick look at the guards inside. His jaw worked, his teeth grinding, a tic of his, a sign of his frustration. "Dammit," he said. "Damn that maniac." I could tell by his expression he found the words inadequate to truly express his feelings on the matter.

"We need to wake up Wilam," I said, "and get this shuttle moving again. There's nothing we can do for them."

"I'm sorry," Jerry said, "but could you move over here? I need to get several shots." He looked like he was about to ask Charles something – maybe to repeat his "Damn that maniac" phrase so they could try to turn

64

it into a tagline or something, but when he got a look at Charles eyes he turned instead to Jack. "Did you get the discovery of the bodies? I want to get an angle from each door and from above, to set the scene."

Jack looked for a moment as if he hadn't heard, then shook himself. "In here you mean? What about security? You want the same for the guards? That room's a little darker but I can change the exposure to make up for it."

"Stop," I said. "Just stop." The door to the security cabin had automatically closed again and now I moved in front of it, barring entry. "We're all going back to the cabin to wait. Charles, I need you and Mike to get Wilam back on his feet so we can get back in motion and alert the authorities." I folded my arms across my chest and waited for them to move, then followed them back through the hall. I was the last one to crawl back through the square in the door and saw they were all now staring out at the window display, distracted by a new object that had appeared in the distance.

"Now that's a law ship," Mike said. "I'm pretty sure that's an inter-cosmic Glinyan assault unit."

Mike tended to be right about that sort of useless info, probably something he had picked up from his game. I didn't know. But it was obviously a law-ship with the standard array of lights moving in the "stay-where-you-are" pattern. Glinyan ships had a very different look than Guvian, it seemed. Whereas the gobo pirate vessel had been formed of blocks stacked upon a platform the Glinyan assault vessel was composed instead of a single large globe with triangles – pyramids, really, sticking out in all directions. It approached slowly and cautiously with still a minute or two left before it reached us.

"I changed my mind," I said. "Mike, you stay here and keep everyone calm. Charles, come with me to the cockpit."

"Why do you think we're not calm?" demanded Jerry.

"Please," I said. "Just wait here."

I waved my hand over the sensor and moved through to the cockpit, allowing Charles to take the lead once we were through the door. It was only a few short steps to the pilot's cabin, a small cubicle with barely enough space for two, all the controls within easy reach of the single chair. Wilam was strapped into it, his head drooping to one side, a headset similar to a cell phone hanging crookedly from one ear. A little line of spittle ran from his mouth to his cheek and we could hear him breathing loudly, almost snoring.

"I tried to wake him," Charles said. "Whatever knocked him out, it was some pretty strong stuff."

I moved behind his chair and carefully removed the headset from his head, slipping it onto my own ear and peering through its digital display lens. An indicator blinked red and I slapped at it, turning it green. Immediately I could hear a voice through the headphones. It sounded like a man speaking gibberish, something with a lot of consonants and not nearly enough vowels.

"Hello?" I said. "I'm sorry, I do not speak Guvian."

The deep voice stopped abruptly, then continued a moment later. Still gibberish. "Anglish?" I said. "I speak Anglish."

After another brief moment of silence I finally heard

something I understood. "Who have I? This is not Wilam Skis sa Skamkam? Please recite your number of registration." Every word was enunciated slowly and clearly with pauses between the phrases as though the speaker was being fed the words from a translator. Apparently they didn't have an officer on board who spoke anglish.

"I don't have a registration number," I said. "The pilot is here. Wilam is here. We've been attacked."

There was a pause on the other end, then the voice picked up again. "We will speak to Wilam Skis, immediately."

"He can't," I said. "We've been attacked, I told you. They knocked him out."

We had a different angle from the display in the cockpit, equally large but more head-on to the approach of the enforcement vessel. As we watched it stopped its motion and the light display changed from the "stay-where-you-are" pattern to the exploding red circle that indicated an emergency situation. A higher level alert, but for us it still meant pretty much the same thing. Stay where you are.

The voice came back to inform us they intended to board. "Please gather all passengers in a single location. Please remove all wearable technology. Please unhand all weaponry. Please keep all limbs visible and empty of any device. Please remove yourself from the cockpit and stay clear of the boarding portal."

"What about the pilot?" I asked.

"Please remove yourself from the cockpit. Please stay clear of the boarding portal."

"Should I leave him here? He's unconscious."

"Please gather all passengers in a single location." I could hear in his voice he was getting irritated with me so I let it go. I stripped off the headset and put it on the console, then led Charles back to the cabin. Once there I repeated the instructions we had been given.

Jack and Jerry exchanged a look.

"I know, you need footage. Listen, leave them recording if you want, that's on you, but don't challenge these guys, okay? They're here to help. Just take off the cells and put them here on the floor."

I threw mine down first as an example, then took off my shoes. Charles did the same, yelling at Mike when he hesitated. "Come on! All limbs visible and empty of device, you heard him!"

In under a minute we were all standing in the center of the cabin, barefooted, hands free, having moved the drink table to create an open space large enough for the five of us to gather. Our cell phones were all on the floor on other side, well out of our reach, with the seats acting as a barrier between.

This is how the guvian law officers found us two minutes later. There were five of them all dressed in combat gear, not too different from what law-men wore back home but all in one piece like a jumpsuit. Unlike an earthen law force there was no consistent uniform. Two wore black but the others were two shades of green and an orange. The only thing the same was that they all wore helmets and thick armor pads that made it impossible to see their faces or make any real sense of their physique.

They entered carefully, coming through the same airlock we had walked through on the ground, slowly entering the room one at a time with firearms in hand. I had no doubt their helmets were also equipped with assault capabilities. The last one to enter waved his hand in a chopping gesture and they all stopped, then he removed his helmet to reveal he was a not a he but a she. Guvian. Long, flowing hair like an Earthen magazine picture. One big, strange, creepy eye covered with a bright yellow lid, the other hidden behind her cell still attached to her head.

She inspected us carefully one by one and head to toe. I was impressed by her thorough patience but I could sense it was making Jack in particular sweat bricks. I wanted to remind him we were the victims, we had nothing to worry about, but truth was she intimidated me too. Or maybe it was the assault weapons. Anyway, I kept my mouth shut.

Finally she spoke in anglish, clearly uncomfortable with forming the words. "We are interested in finding out who has disabled the pilot. Why are there less passengers than on the manifest? We will take one statement. It must be brief. Who will make it?" This seemed a prepared translation. She breathed a sigh of relief when she finished so I assumed my entire statement would be tediously fed through a translation app on her cell and probably recorded for later analysis.

"We have been attacked," I said, "and some of our party has been kidnapped. Others have been killed. We have left all the deceased as we found them." I could have said more, but the purpose of our trip was a part of the manifest. I assumed they knew why we were here.

I waited as she worked on a translation, all of us

69

tensely silent, the other four law officers like statues with their weapons trained relentlessly on us. Better safe than sorry, I guess, but it felt rough, all of us already shook up being treated like the bad guys. No sense of sympathy came through the thick security helmets.

As she listened to the translation app — which none of us could hear, of course — she took her time examining the room. The three laser cutouts were of particular interest, it seemed. First she checked out the panel over the service door, then the square I had cut through to the passageway, and finally Charles' unfinished circle on the other door. She waved at the others to lower the firearms, though they all still stood attentive and at the ready. She then gave instructions in guvian to one of the other officers who moved to the pile of cell phones and began going through them. "We are sorry for your loss," she told us. No doubt this had been offered by her translation app as the appropriate social nicety. "Show me the deceased, please," she said to me. "Others, remain here."

I nodded and climbed through into the short passageway between cabins. She followed and I walked her through the same gruesome discoveries I had made only minutes ago.

It was interesting to watch her make her inspection, her eyelids flicking, sometimes rapidly, between a number of different *shatia*. I tried counting but I couldn't really keep up. It seemed like she must have at least eight or nine.

As she knelt by the two bodies in the coach cabin — Gina and her assistant Susan from the 3V crew — she gave me a puzzled look and consulted again with her translator.

"You did not inform others were as well unawake."

"What?" I said, a step slow in making sense of the bad translation.

"The pilot unawake. Also these. Where are the deceased?"

I shook my head, confused. "They are deceased."

"No," she said. "She breathe."

"What?" I said. "That's impossible." I stepped closer to check for myself but she raised a hand in warning, the other dropping to the firearm at her hip. "Sorry," I said, backing off.

She spoke in guvian, calling one of the others on her cell I assumed, though her eyes never left me and her hand never left her weapon. She then carefully moved Susan's body from atop Gina's so that they were side by side. I offered to help — it didn't look easy — but she gave me a warning look and I left it. When she was finished she checked something on her cell — or so I gathered from a series of quick hand gestures — then began loosening the clothing around the women's collars. Both the director and her assistant had been wearing the same sort of high throated jacket, magnetic buttons all the way up to the chin. I could see now from where I stood how Gina's chest rose and fell — she was indeed alive. How had I missed it?

I remembered then the attendants who had been left the same way. "The others," I said, pointing at the service door. "They may be alive too. Unconscious?" I said. "I don't know how it's possible. I thought they were dead. Maybe it was some kind of drug?" I was thinking of Shakespeare, Romeo and Juliet, something like that. Had our madman used a poison that slowed their metabolism, left them in a comatose state?

The law officer looked at me through three consecutive shades of *shatia* then slowly approached the service door. She opened it with the automatic sensor and waved me through first. I guess she wanted to keep an eye on me.

On the other side Adula still lay atop Ruisha as though whoever had arranged them was trying to save on floor space. I saw no indication they were alive, but I stood well back and let the officer check. I could tell from her expression they were fine. She moved Adula, though in this case there was no need to loosen any clothing as both had been wearing very revealing tops already. Instead the guvian officer took a moment to check their pulses, pressing against each of their necks for fifteen or twenty seconds, no doubt timing it with her cell. She looked up when the door opened and two of the other officers joined us. One had removed his helmet and the two exchanged brief incomprehensible dialogue.

"Come," she then said to me, and we went back through to the coach cabin. "Here?" she said before opening the security door. "Unawake? Or deceased?"

"Deceased," I said. I didn't see how they could not be.

She did not make me follow her this time, but instead left me standing there as the other two officers moved back and forth between coach and service cabin, administering to the unconscious as best they could, carefully moving them from the floor to the couches, elevating their heads slightly with pillows.

"Are they okay?" I asked, but they ignored me. I was

sure they had all the latest medical sensors on their helmets at least, if not built into their cells, but they had taken mine and all I could do was watch. A moment later the first officer returned from the security cabin, shaking her head grimly.

"Deceased," she told me. She spoke to the other officers and both disappeared into the security cabin. She turned back to me and gave me a long look, again flipping through a series of *shatia*. It was disconcerting; I'd come later to learn it was common in gobo interaction and eventually get used to it but right then as rattled as I was already it made my stomach turn, whether with nervousness or disgust it was hard to say.

"What now?" I said, because I don't like tension.

"Do not resist," she said, and I didn't as she grabbed both my wrists – gently – and secured them behind my back with some sort of rubber wrist-cuffs. At least they felt like rubber. As quickly as she moved I never got a look at them.

"You come with us," she said. "We talk to you at our base."

I sighed. "Yeah, I guess. What choice do I have?" But I stopped before we went back through the passageway. "But you need to send someone after those murderers. They have taken India Phoenix."

She nudged me forward, her expression never changing. "We will talk to you at our base."

73

····6····

SIX HOURS LATER THEY FINALLY RELEASED US. It was a grueling experience but they did not treat us badly. They were thorough, clinical, and professional. I had worked with enough behavior enforcement on Earth to see that procedurally it wasn't that different though we were never offered access to counsel.

They kept us all in separate rooms, tiny cells with chairs, cots, and toilet facilities but nothing else. I waited quietly, staring at the red light above the door since there was nothing else to look at.

I think they interrogated me last. I waited a long time at the beginning, several hours at least, though I didn't have any real way of tracking the time. It was an agonizing period of interminable thinking which I will not bore you with but understand I had no idea what to expect, and the worse the possibility I considered the more time I spent perversely fleshing out its reality. Finally the light turned green, the door swooshed open, and a white-shirted gobo who looked too skinny to be a law officer led me into another room where three much heftier gobos waited at a table.

74

These guys would have been intimidating even if they were trying to be friendly, which they weren't. But the questioning was straightforward enough and I answered everything honestly — including a very uncomfortable moment when they threw my cell phone down on the table and asked me about my laser application.

I should mention here that two of the gobos did all the talking, and they were excellent — and I mean excellent — in their anglish, and the other seemed to follow without a problem. Maybe it was a mistake to try to read their body language the way I would a human but I couldn't help it, and they certainly seemed humanlike in their activity. The silent one hardly moved, keeping one hand thoughtfully at his chin, his eyes never leaving me. If I had found the single officer fluttering her *shatia* at me nerve-wracking what can I say about these three, with me in the bright interrogation light and them half in shadow, glittering their pupil-less, ambiguous screens above eerily human snarls and frowns, wringing my own words around my neck like piano wire? I was a gibbering mess and frankly I'm glad they didn't let the 3V crew in to catch any of it.

Anyway, I threw Charles under the bus. This seemed like the right approach. I figured Charles had told the truth and it was up to him to explain where he got the app. In the end this proved the most difficult part of the interview — or interrogation, it's hard to say which — and my answers must have gibed with everyone else's. So finally, they released us.

"Vavaka as'Tatim has come personally to receive you," one of them told me, which from the way he said it I took to be a great honor. Then the silent one led me down the hall to a waiting room where the others were all seated. By others, I mean everyone including the pilot, the flight attendants, and the 3V crew, who all looked exhausted. Jack and Jerry started filming the moment I came through the door and Charles and Mike both stood up like they had been expecting me.

"Finally!" said Mike.

"How did it go?" said Charles. "They just told us to come in here and wait."

I was about to answer when a door on the opposite side of the room opened and a small procession of people came in, mostly gobos but led by a human who was looking right at me.

"Mr. Lewis! We are so sorry you have been embroiled in this disaster." I shook his outstretched hand, a firm but friendly exchange, and looked past him to a figure I recognized from my dossier. The human saw my glance and immediately stepped to the side. "Allow me to introduce his excellency Vavaka as'Tatim."

Vavaka was shorter than I had expected – about my own height – and wore a long robe, his hands clasped behind him. He inspected me with yellow *shatia* that faded to orange at the edges. His, unlike all the others, stayed steady, never flickering to another.

I stepped forward and offered him my hand. He regarded it for a moment then grasped it briefly and politely.

"My name is Offman," said the human, slipping between us. "Yuli Offman. Please, call me Yuli. I will be translating for Vavaka when necessary and I can also serve as a guide for you and your team while you are here."

"Our pleasure to meet you both," I said, trying to diplomatically speak for the group. "We appreciate the hospitality."

"I thought his excellency spoke anglish," said Charles rudely, but the translator grinned.

"I do," said Vavaka, giving him a cold look.

"Please," said Yuli, "allow us to take you to your rooms. His excellency is most upset about this tragedy and as soon as you are rested we will discuss our options. His excellency is obviously very disturbed by the kidnapping of his fiancé and desires no delay. Please, we have a taxi waiting. We are not far from the estate."

This was directed at me, but I turned to look at the others to see what they thought. Everybody looked tired, especially the five who had been found unconscious.

I really wanted to interview them myself, to be honest, since as yet no one had shared their account of the experience with me. I hoped Charles had gotten a chance to feel them out a little bit since it seemed I would have scant opportunity.

"What about medical attention?" I asked the translator. "I'm fine. We weren't personally attacked, but what about the others? Have they been checked out?"

"They have been examined by the *halikari*," said Yuli. "Our medical scans indicate that they were anesthetized with a light tranquilizer, nothing that will do any permanent damage. After you have all rested we will be happy to share everything we know."

Vavaka leaned in to murmur something to him, then quietly left the room, never looking back at us. The procession that had entered with him followed, all except Yuli who waited for us patiently.

"We had baggage," I said, "on the shuttle."

"Yes," said Yuli. "I'm sure it has been taken care of."

The pilot, Wilam, looked up, his face slack and devoid of energy. "The baggage was stolen. All of it, taken."

Yuli lowered his eyebrows, frowning. "I am most sorry, I was unaware."

"You mean those bastards took all our stuff?" said Charles. Then he sighed like he didn't have the energy to be upset. "I guess it doesn't matter. I didn't pack anything important."

"At least they gave us back our cells," said Mike, and I nodded agreement. I had been a little worried about it — all the questioning regarding the laser app had concerned me — but one of the officers had handed it back after the interview without saying anything else about it.

I put the cell on as we followed Yuli to a taxi. I checked to see if the laser app was still installed — it was — and to see if I had any new messages. I did. Too many. Over two hundred. Most of them were probably just junk my spam filter had missed, but any of them could be important. I took a seat next to Charles in the cab and started to go through them.

You might think, by the way, the taxi was something like you might find in an earthen polyplex, but you'd be wrong. The translator called it a taxi for the same reason I called it a cab — because that's what you took to get from place to place in the city — but I would have called this, colloquially, a "limousine," and still that would have given the wrong impression. Get the image of a stretch shuttle out of your mind and instead picture a floating room with carpets and picture windows and you'd get more of the idea. The seat I took next to Charles was a cushioned recliner, comfortable enough I almost fell asleep before I opened even the first message.

It was a credit offer. I deleted it and also the next two, a museum membership renewal and an advertisement for some new mental ability mod promising permanent increased intellection for half the price of a university degree. Delete, delete, delete, delete, delete, then finally one was legit, a vid from my brother asking if I had arrived all right. He was worried since he hadn't heard from us on schedule. I deleted it too. I knew Mike would have given him a rough update right away.

Indeed a new message from Lewis came shortly before we arrived at Vavaka's estate with the subject "Call me now!!!"

Since I made it a policy to never respond immediately to multiple explanation points I waited until we had been shown to our rooms. Then I steeled myself and told my phone, "Call Lewis."

I waited. Our service was provided by Liotek alien technology so the communication delay between systems was a very manageable nine seconds. I believe our videos were literally being sent back in time to accomplish the feat. Still even the slight delay grew pretty annoying over the course of a long conversation. The same could be said of Lewis so I tried to keep the whole thing as short as possible. He started talking the moment he answered, but I interrupted.

"Lewis. Lewis! Slow down, please slow down. I'm very tired."

Nine seconds later he looked taken aback, then to his credit a rare bit of empathy set in and he took a closer look at me. His cell as usual was sitting on his desk but I could see his profile clearly in the upper right corner, his gaze directed somewhere to my left. He must have been watching me on the big screen. "Are you all right? Mike said you weren't hurt."

"Tired, Lewis," I said. "I'm just tired. It's been a very long trip so far."

"I can imagine," he said. "Well I haven't had a chance to talk to Vavaka yet, just his assistant, but I've got the Phoenix family all over me here. They want to know what's going on."

"I don't think anyone knows yet," I said.

"We can't have that," he said. "We have to be on top of this."

"So far it seems like the *halikari* are as on top of it as anyone can be."

"*Halikari*?" he repeated. Apparently he'd never heard the word.

"Local behavior enforcement," I explained. "You are aware we've been in their custody, right? Mike told you that?"

"He said you'd been interviewed by the cops, yes." He frowned. "Listen, I don't think the Phoenixes would be very happy if we lost control of this so whatever's going on with the *haliaki—*"

"*Halikari.*"

"you need to keep me updated." He came over to the

desk and looked directly into the cell, his brow furrowed anxiously. "This is a disaster! You know that, right? We've lost India Phoenix!" He was so close now I could clearly see that he was wearing cosmetics, an affectation he had started since becoming a reality star.

"Your foundation doesn't quite match your skin color," I told him. He kept going but nine seconds later it hurt his feelings and I felt bad. "I'm sorry," I said. "I'm just tired. Look, let me get a little rest and I will give you a full update, okay?"

He sighed. "Yeah, fine. Call me before you do anything else."

I hung up and sat down heavily in a recliner opposite what looked like a giant 3V screen. Both recliner and screen curved to follow the contour of the wall. The chair immediately adjusted itself to fit my form a little better and I leaned gratefully into its soft folds.

While the estate outside our suite was decidedly guvian the suite itself was clearly intended for earthen guests. Whether Vavaka entertained a lot of earthen guests or whether he had enough money to set it up just for us I didn't know but everything was top of the line, luxurious and comfortable, most of it probably imported directly from Earth. The whole room taken together was also ugly as sin, ostentatious, everything done in gold and glass and glittering like a princess tiara. Personally I liked dark blues, purples and blacks. Bright lights and colors tended to give me a headache.

I asked the room to dim the light to about twenty percent and immediately the bright glitters of gold subsided to gentle highlights. Much better, I thought, my last conscious tendril before drifting off to sleep

81

right there in the recliner.

I dreamed, I know, of the kidnapping, reliving it over. Some things were changed. In my dream the killer cut through the door with the laser on my cell phone app and his voice was the same but in the dream he was a giant worm with great yellow eyes and huge shark teeth. "309J236!" he screamed. "309J236?!" I thought he was demanding some kind of answer but I didn't have one.

Vavaka's estate spread over a good portion of the northern part of Jebala which in turn lie at the very southern tip of Parshun, the nation-state that governed the area. We had only seen the city from above as we flew from the station but what I saw resonated with the memory of my sim experience. Dark to my human eyes, I had adjusted the exposure on my cell to make up for it. Geometric grids rose out of the landscape in patterns that reminded me of hieroglyphics or pictograms, some early undiscovered alphabet writ large upon the city. We flew high enough to see the empty expanse of desert that dominated the south, though I knew a variety of ecosystems existed just below. While gobos had adjusted to life on the surface and lived there comfortably for over two thousand years their lives still extended deeply underground and an estate like Vavaka's probably extended kilometers below the surface.

We approached from the sky, following a single elevated road below that approached the giant wall surrounding the aboveground living quarters. Guards watched us pass when we flew over, which I thought curious as Jebala was hardly known for violence. A series of domes just outside the walls could conceivably have been some kind of housing; servants quarters I guessed as I couldn't imagine who else might want to live directly under the sights of such guards.

Once we were taken inside the translator Offman gave us a brief tour of our suite, which included a dining room, a library, an entertainment lounge, and our rooms, spaced evenly around the outside of the common area. Offman called it the "West Wing" but don't get notions of an earthen mansion, an ancient imperial plantation or some such thing. Despite the imported earthen furniture the structure of Vavaka's estate was entirely guvian. Where we might expect rooms shaped like squares and boxes on Asitot more natural flowing forms were preferred, free of corners and construction lines. Imagine yourself in a sumptuously decorated, electrically lit cave with passageways leading to caverns of all different sizes and you'll get more of the idea. I could see where it would be very easy for a human to get lost over the whole estate, though our suite was straightforward enough. It just took getting used to as it followed none of our linear earthen conventions.

I don't know about the others but my own room was constructed in the shape of an egg. Even the floor was curved. It felt weird to walk on it. But everything already felt a little weird even without that. The gravity was slightly off, the atmosphere was too thin, and the air was so dry it hummed with static. Every motion felt clumsy. It was hard to breathe and I was always thirsty.

It seemed like my tongue was constantly searching my mouth for water.

I called Lewis after I had some breakfast and juice – I was able to sneak out and grab some fruit without running in to anyone else – and he answered immediately. I hadn't checked to see what time it was back home but he was wearing a soft blue bathrobe, which meant it was probably the middle of the night.

"I didn't wake you up, did I?" I asked, hoping I had.

"There's no time for that," he said.

"What, sleeping?"

"Listen, it's pretty tense here, okay? I need you to call Debra Rhine immediately, I already forwarded her contact to you. Don't wait. Any time–"

"Isn't it pretty late there?"

"day or night, she said. The Phoenix family is worried, you understand? Worried sick."

"I do understand," I said. "*I'm* worried and I barely know her."

"Listen, between you and me," and here he dropped his voice to an intense whisper, "this is one of those disasters that could turn out to be very good for us. Forget Vavaka, okay? You need to find this kidnapper and rescue India Phoenix, you understand? You realize if you save India Phoenix's life what that means for me? We're talking India Phoenix."

Obviously. "You realize," I said, "if this kidnapper kills her, what *that* does to your reputation?"

"You don't think he's going to kill her, do you? It's a ransom, right?" Lewis looked worried.

"He killed several people already. He's a psychopath, Lewis. Ransom? Maybe money is the motive. All I know is the guy is a madman."

He shook his head, frowning. "Look, just call Debra Rhine. I'm counting on you, okay?"

"Yeah, okay."

I disconnected and called Debra Rhine. I checked Earth time zone 6 first — I didn't want to be rude — and saw it was late in the morning. She didn't answer quite as quickly as Lewis had but when she did she seemed fully awake and alert. She demanded a full account of our journey so far and asked several detailed questions about the events on the shuttle. It seemed I was just confirming things she already knew. When I finished she nodded once, quickly, precisely.

"Don't worry," she said, "I don't expect you or your team to find India. Your assignment has not changed. You will continue to investigate Vavaka's background."

"You think the two are related?"

She looked at me like I was an idiot. "Vavaka and this kidnapping? I do not." She paused. It seemed like she was thinking about something so I kept my mouth shut. After a moment she said, "But if you find anything questionable in your investigations of his background, you will let us know immediately. We have no reason whatsoever to believe Vavaka was in any way behind this and have no intention of insulting his name with that insinuation, you understand?"

"Of course."

"We are following up other leads from here."

"You think it's the stalker?" I said. "The one who's been harassing her?"

She gave me a sharp look. "What do you know of this?"

"She mentioned someone," I said. "In passing."

"What did she say?"

"She didn't know him. A gamer, I think."

"We are aware of this individual and are following up on it," she said, her tone dismissive. "We will also be sending a team to the Pyramus station but they will not interfere with your work. Please continue to focus on the background of Vavaka as'Tatim. This current situation is unfortunate but unrelated to your current agenda. In particular I would like to know his financial status, his business affiliations, and his family background, much of which is not on record."

"It will be challenging to investigate Vavaka when he is my host," I said. "With all our arrangements being handled by his people don't you think he's going to know everything I find out?"

She nodded. "Indeed. It was my intention to have our security keep an eye on you. I will send replacements. Until they arrive please just do your best. Please understand, Mr. Gregory, I do not expect you to find anything untoward. We have done our own work from here and all we expect is that you verify that which we already know. I will send a dossier with your security detail."

After we disconnected I thought about the two requests – Lewis's and Ms. Rhine's – and how it seemed I had been given conflicting orders. I considered calling Lewis back but decided against. Truth was I was more interested in what happened to India than in Vavaka's background and – like Ms. Rhine – I thought the two were unrelated. All except the timing. But no doubt India's stalker had seized on the opportunity of her travel.

Why waste my time on Vavaka? It was a routine checkup. Merely a formality. No one had any real reason to think there was anything to be concerned about. I would keep my eyes and ears open but I knew already most of my attention would be consumed with finding India. It pained me to think it but on this occasion I agreed with my brother.

Anyway, after thinking over things for a while I got dressed and stepped out of my room. My phone told me it was 14:14, still earthen time. It had been about six hours since we arrived, then, but the time meant nothing here. It would take me a little while to adjust to the Asitot cycle.

I heard conversation in the dining area so I stepped around that way and found Charles and Mike having an argument. Mike cut off in mid-sentence when he saw me, looking guilty.

"What were you saying?" I asked him.

"We were just talking about the... on the shuttle."

Charles twisted his mouth quizzically and pointed his thumb at Mike. "He was wondering how the creep knew you."

I looked at Mike but his eyes were busy on the table. "Who, the killer? India's kidnapper?" I asked. "He doesn't know me."

Mike shrugged but didn't look up. "I wasn't saying you knew him or anything, sir." Mike had called me that ever since our first job together, same as he called Lewis. I had tried to get him to quit but he was stubborn. "I was just asking Mr. Thomas how he knew all that stuff about you."

"He didn't know anything about me," I said. "That was all bluff."

"He seemed to." Now Mike glanced up to see how I was taking it and I saw right away he was worried about things he didn't know how to think about.

"We're going to get him, Mike," I said to reassure him, but then I saw him wince and the look of consternation that came over his face and fixed it. "I mean the *halikari* will. Lewis told you we're going to focus on Vavaka, right? That's what we're going to do. But the *halikari* will catch him."

"He might know things about all of us," Mike said gloomily.

"It was a bluff," I said again. Then, to get his mind on something else: "You were saying something about the time here, how they break up the day into quarter-turns. Is that right?"

"Yeah," he said. "I set my phone to it earlier."

"Good," I said. "We should probably all do that. What time is it?"

He checked his cell. "It's almost third quarter. They call that one *bazza*."

That resonated in my memory somewhere but I didn't go searching for it. Instead I asked, "Explain. What happens then?"

He blinked at me, wide-eyed.

Charles said, "Is it like morning? Noon? Lunch time?"

"Oh," he said. "They should be getting up soon, I think. We're in *shumbo* now. Solitary time. Mostly I think it's for sleeping. But *bazza* is fun time." His brow furrowed as he scratched for what this really meant. "It's like twelve hours of partying?"

I flipped to the time setting on my phone and changed it to local time. It showed a graph approximately halfway full and a countdown in front of a star. As I watched, it went from "754" to "753" to "752."

"This display makes no sense to me," Charles said.

"We would say in translation, it is 'less 8 cents to *bazza*,'" said a voice from behind us, and we all jumped. Yulie Offman, the translator, watched us from the other side of the lounge. "*Bazza* translates not well as 'party time.' You will see no parties in the manner you are thinking. In fact these would be quite offensive. There is no real translation for *bazza*. It is a time when we on Asitot focus on our health, our families, our development. It is a personal time where we respect the privacy of the activities of others and a spiritual time for those who believe in things of the spirit. It is best not to bother one in his activities during *bazza*."

I thought about that for a second. "So there's no itinerary then? What are we to do during *bazza*?"

"Vavaka will see you if you wish. He understands the human customs. But it is usual to wait until after *bazza* for business matters."

"Even in matters of life and death?" Charles asked, an intimidating furrow to his brow.

"It is usual," said Offman. "But as I said, Vavaka appreciates the Earthen ways and is willing to see you if requested. I encourage you, however, to focus on your own *bazza*, which you see is not merely a time of day but also a most important state of mind. I myself will not be available for translations as I have much to dwell on." He nodded sharply at us. "Blessings on your *bazza*."

"Likewise," I said. He left and the three of us looked at each other.

"So what are we supposed to do for twelve hours?" said Charles.

I didn't have an answer and was saved from making one by the appearance of Jack, blinking at us blearily like he had just rolled out of bed.

"Where's Jerry?" he said. "One of us should be filming." He felt at his eye but his cell wasn't there. He looked confused and shook his head. "I'll go get my camera."

"Don't bother," I said. "It's just over 5 cents to *bazza*."

Charles, who appreciated my sense of humor, smirked, but we both underestimated Jack.

"Yes of course," he said. "I'm willing to work though. I don't have any personal business here anyway, right? Jerry signed off on it too."

"You know *bazza*?" Mike asked.

"It's in our contracts," said Jack. "We're part of the guild, you know."

"The union," Charles said.

"It's not a union," Jack stated firmly. "It's a guild." I waved aside this political argument as these things never went anywhere.

"Take the *bazza* off," I said. "Or if you'd rather you can work on some editing or something. But respect *our* privacy, if you don't mind."

He looked a little wounded but shrugged it off. "Fine," he said. "No big deal. But remember you told us to so we still get paid."

"Unions," said Charles.

I gave him a look and reassured Jack. "Of course. I'll

clear all that with Lewis later."

Jack didn't go back to his room right away though, but instead regarded us for a long moment. "I don't really have anything to do," he said. "You don't really mind if I hang out with you guys, do you? I won't film it or anything."

"Of course not," said Mike, apparently thinking he spoke for all of us.

"Nice," said Jack. "I'm going to take a shower." He went back into his room and I frowned at Mike.

"You guys have a good time," I said. "I've got some business to take care of." I didn't know what it was yet but I kept that to myself.

"It's *bazza*," Mike protested.

"Yes," I said. "It's personal business." I left the table and went back to my own room, waited five minutes and called Charles. He answered, having already escaped Mike's clutches.

"I'm back in my room," he said.

"Perfect," I said. "Meet me out front in fifteen minutes."

"Got it," he said, then before he hung up he said, "How do you get outside? Do you know?" He looked abashed. Charles didn't like asking for help. In this case, I couldn't help anyway.

"No idea," I said. "I guess we've got fifteen minutes to figure it out."

"What is that in cents?" he asked, and a half-second later our phones informed us both. 17 cents. 1700 clicks. This was going to take some major getting used to.

"See you in 17," I said, and disconnected.

·····7·····

FIFTEEN MINUTES LATER I STEPPED OUT of the tunnel that
served as the north entryway into the dim light of the
Asitot day. Charles was already waiting, sitting on a
rock that was probably intended as a bench as it
overlooked a lovely garden with a tiny fountain and an
arrangement of sculpted stones. As a bench it was
lacking – the rock was hard and uncomfortable and not
shaped well for my human posterior – but I sat next to
Charles anyway and we chatted idly for a bit, enjoying
the quiet outdoors and the break from the others. For
much of the year Asitot's surface was too hot to be
outdoors but we had come in its mildest season and the
weather wasn't too different from the Dallas-Houston
area.

Charles and I talked about our usual things: politics,
earthen news and gossip, sports, and so on. By some
unspoken agreement we pushed all other worries aside
and enjoyed ourselves for a bit.

At *bazza* the large orange sun hung atop a mint green
sky like a giant full moon, dim enough it seemed you
could look right at it if you didn't care about your long-

term vision. It seemed like autumn but that was earthen sensibilities. Asitot's limited surface plant life just photosynthesized a different spectrum. What grass and weeds clumped through the sandy ground were vibrant orange instead of Earthen green. Isolated trees in the distance, scattered like sentries around the perimeter, rose from short black trunks to arcing leaves of burnt umbers and blood reds. But above all Asitot was a rocky, sandy, bare and ugly surface.

Only in the garden did the colors range more deeply and I saw as I sat there how artfully it had been arranged to highlight blues, purples, and greens that must have been gathered from all over Asitot if not beyond. I was impressed. My experience of the planet in sim had been almost entirely underground and I had honestly thought Asitot incapable of even this simple beauty. Here in this spot it was somehow more earthen than I would have expected.

Eventually Charles turned our conversation to business with the question, "So why did you want to meet outside?"

I sat up straighter, shaking out of my relaxed languor, but took a moment before answering. I looked around at the garden. Up at the sky.

"Satellites," he said, before I had spoken. "Can't see them from here but sure they're up there." He had pegged my hesitation. I was considering the possibility of surveillance.

"Nothing like in the house or in the tunnels," I said. I didn't know if we were being spied on but it seemed good practice to assume the worst. I had no reason to trust Vavaka or his staff. I stood up and said, "Walk with me." Charles followed me from the garden down a path that led around the estate and eventually to the road that went out through the front gate. Though most of the transportation happened underground, Asitot did have surface roads. This particular one served almost as a personal driveway for Vavaka. I imaged he connected to the city in other ways underground. "Do you think," I asked when I had put some space between us and the manor, "that our investigation of Vavaka and the attack on the shuttle are related?" Charles followed slightly behind me. I had to peek over my left shoulder as I said the words.

He didn't hesitate. "Related? Yes. I think somehow they're related." He stepped a little quicker, keeping pace so we could converse while walking. The brick path was just wide enough for the two of us.

"You think Vavaka's behind it?"

This time he took a second. "I didn't say that. I don't know how that would make sense really. You could say the timing is a coincidence but... I'm not much for coincidences."

"Me either," I said, but they did happen all the time. I couldn't completely rule them out.

Charles voiced some of my other thoughts. "The kidnapper knew we were going to be there. Had to, right? He knew the ship would be there and he knew who was going to be on it. He seemed to know everything he needed to about the shuttle. Was any of that public record? Where did he get all this information?"

I nodded, frowning. "Exactly."

"So maybe it's an inside job, right? We can rule out

Mike and we can rule out Lewis and I don't see what the camera crew would have to do with it. Maybe it's Vavaka or maybe somebody associated with Vavaka. Or maybe somebody from the Phoenix family. Maybe a jealous lover, something like that." He thought it over and shook his head. "But it seems more likely it's some kind of tech wiz, maybe someone who hacked India's cell or into our itinerary. Which means discard all that, it's maybe *not* an inside job at all. Isn't that what you're thinking?"

"Yeah, that's what I'm thinking." I confirmed. I told him what little I knew about India's previous trouble — some unnamed stalker, a fellow gamer or something. Hacking throughout civilization was considered both piracy and privacy invasion and was taken very seriously, since everyone in the universe relied heavily on reliable tech. Even small-time hacking could get you eliminated and civilization for the most part leaned heavily against the elimination of enemies. Hacking, in short, was among the worst of crimes. Still, obsession being what it was virtual stalking would never disappear completely.

"That's interesting," he said. "You think she told Vavaka about that?"

"She's planning on marrying him. I would think so." Though truthfully I didn't think it necessarily meant anything like that. I had my doubts about how deep the relationship really went.

"But her family knows."

I nodded. "I have been told they are handling that end," I told him. "I'm supposed to focus on Vavaka."

"But maybe the two are related," he said. "I see. You

just need justification."

"Exactly," I nodded. "That's why I'm going to have you look into the hacker side. And I need you to find a reason to be doing so."

"A gaming stalker." He nodded thoughtfully. "He must be good too, the way he handled our shuttle so easily. And to be hacking India Phoenix? He must have both talent and chutz. I guess I have to be careful what I search." His forehead crunched uncomfortably as he considered the ramifications. "And on a foreign planet where I don't know half of what anything is? That's not going to be easy."

"You need to research. We can't assume a hacker is monitoring our every wiki question," I said. "Just keep it light and ambiguous and stay anonymous wherever possible. Do what you can during *bazza* when there's no camera crew too, since there's the possibility someone's monitoring the footage. I'll try to keep them following me the rest of the time. I should be back well before the end of *bazza*."

"Yeah," he said, shaking his head. "I'll try to keep a low profile but you know that's hard for me." He laughed, then bumped my fist and turned back toward the estate. "I'll get to the web immediately. See what I can find out generically speaking. I'll let you know what I got when you get back."

"Sure," I said, and couldn't help adding, "but time is of the essence." The occasional hyperbolic cliché made me feel important and I really didn't think I was overstating it. The attacker – stalker, kidnapper, hacker – was obviously following a plan and from his vague threats it seemed it had a few parts left to completion.

I intended to interrupt them before it reached that point, but who knew how long that would be?

I sighed, accepting the difficult reality: so far I still knew nothing about what was going on. All I had were speculations. Of course it wasn't really my job — my job was background on Vavaka — but I wasn't going to let that get in my way either.

As Charles headed back to the mansion I continued the other way, walking toward the gate that exited the estate. I had looked over some maps of the area and knew we were only about eight kilometers away from the nearest *pedto*, which my phone translated — terribly — as "suburb" but which was more like a downtown main street, a community center above the town, which itself existed mostly underground. The *pedto* looked easy to find from the map and I decided to hoof it rather than be so rude as to rustle up a taxi during *bazza*. I really didn't know for sure but I had gotten the impression I was supposed to bother as few gobos as possible.

As I neared the gate though I saw the guards still at their posts. Three of them watched me silently as I approached. I raised a hand in friendly greeting but none returned it. Before I was within speaking distance one moved to press a button then waved me through as the gate slowly opened. If they thought my notion to take a long walk an odd one they gave no sign.

Once through the gate the road turned to the right, widening into a deep industrial cleft set into the ground. It was about twelve meters wide, coated with a shiny black metal pavement that had no sympathy for my feet. After a short while I stepped up to the orange grass instead, walking beside the road instead of on it. I enjoyed walking in general and enjoyed this walk especially as everything about the day — literally everything — was splendidly new to me.

The grass eventually gave way to sand. I recalled the flight above the estate and how the color of the landscape had changed as we approached. It was cultivated, I realized. Asitot was a desert planet and the grass only stretched as far as water could be provided. I saw no sign of irrigation but presumed they handled it with piping from below.

The grass was odd besides just the color, curling at the tip into little spirals that gave it a springier, spongier quality than that back home. Did I mention the sand was yellow? And I don't mean tannish brown earthy yellow, I mean like neon bright, brighter than sunflowers and dandelions. I knew the intense color wasn't really the sand, per se — it was a bacteria that permeated the uppermost layer. I had read that if you were lost in the desert you could — as a last resort — suck the nutrient straight out of the sand. The pedias called it "sand plankton" and it somehow survived on the minimal sunlight and air.

Speaking of sunlight and air, there wasn't much of either and it wasn't long before I found myself gasping for breath. The walk seemed longer than I had expected but then I rarely pedaled 8km and the landscape was after a certain point not much to look at. The sun hung dimly above, the ground glowed its mustard glow and ahead the road pointed a black arrow to the horizon.

Twice vehicles rolled past. Rugged work vehicles with two wheels in front, one in back. The first had a lone driver who lifted his hand in a rolling wave that I awkwardly returned. The second was operated by a similarly grizzly driver and carried in addition two young scrappers on the back, standing and holding on for dear life. One of them yelled something at me, a grin on his face, but even had I understood him the driver didn't slow enough for me to make a reply.

Eventually I reached the crest of a dune and found myself looking down on the village laid out in the valley on the other side. It appeared suddenly, almost magically, like an oasis, and I stopped to look at it. My cell had assured me the market operated during *bazza* and I saw in the center of the *pedto* tents and food carts with gobos standing and walking around. The road continued into a tunnel that went underneath it, coming out, I presumed on the other side. Around the market mound-like buildings ran in rows like an irregular wall.

I stopped, a bit intimidated even though I was still probably a half km away. I had roughly memorized the map. I knew the road looped around the *pedto* and that the road on the other side — which led to the city — would be much busier. Vavaka's estate was isolated by design it seemed and there would be little reason for anyone else to go back the way I had come. Another road broke off on the north side and led to the Burrows, the translated name my phone gave to the area of caves where most of these gobos actually lived.

"Suburb" seemed an especially bad translation once you'd seen it. Though Earth had very little in the way of rural communities left this is what it most reminded me of. An old desert town. 3V was full of historical dramas and the way the *pedto* was laid out seemed like something you might see in an old Western.

I continued down the road and after a bit I could tell that I'd been seen, though no one offered any greeting. As I came nearer I saw that the gobos out in the market were all silent, engaged in their own tasks. I saw no conversations or socialization. I had not really known what I expected when I left Vavaka's estate but I had downloaded a comprehensive translator in the hopes of gathering some information — with the phone offline, of course. *Bazza*, I thought, meant a period free of work, but the gobos in the *pedto* did not seem like they were on siesta, they seemed instead to be avoiding any interaction.

I came to where the road turned sharply down and started to descend into the tunnel and stepped instead to the path that led to the market. The small sign on the building to my left translated as "Infrastructure Paradigm," which meant nothing to me, and the stubby, mud-brick mound on the right was labeled "Suburban Military," though the two vehicles — flyers — parked outside were both small sedans and didn't seem especially dangerous. At best it was the town police and I figured I would probably be giving the translation app a pretty bad rating when I went back online. If it struggled with the written text I couldn't imagine it would do too great a job with the spoken language. I could always go back to the built-in translator, I thought, but I hadn't downloaded the full guvian pack before going offline.

Anyway, neither building showed the least sign of activity so I crossed the street and ascended the ramp into the main market. I say "market" because it seemed stuff was for sale and I just don't have a better word to describe it. I thought back on my sim experience, my brief outing as a street painter. The environment looked similar but that had been crowded, active, full of chatter. Here the gobos studiously avoided eye contact and went about their business. It must be because it's *bazza*, I thought, or perhaps the sim had been an inauthentic experience adjusted for the gaming platform. Or maybe it was just this local community wasn't very friendly.

Out of the corner of my eye I could see one or two of the gobos watching me as I walked by but no one greeted me or even acknowledged my presence. All wore the same style of clothing – both men and women in tightly wound cloth wraps that reminded me of old mummy movies except instead of white the gobos wore a variety of patterns and colors. I didn't see any wearing cells. They could have been carrying them somewhere, there's all kinds of styles for cell devices, but I saw no sign of any and in fact I saw hardly any technology at all. The whole vibe was very last millennium. I felt a bit out of place with my own cell on my eye but I didn't think I could get by without it. If any of them did talk to me it would have to provide a translation.

But the longer I walked among the shops in the center the more I became convinced they were all deliberately avoiding me. I didn't think it was just because I was human either. I thought maybe it had something to do with Vavaka, that somehow they knew of me through his reputation. Of course they must have heard of the kidnapping of Vavaka's fiancé unless they didn't follow news and gossip like humans did and that didn't seem likely.

About midway down the market I found a shop I was actually interested in, a small tent that carried actual books. Most were guvian — heavy things with covers made of engraved stone and thin sheets of strange blue paper accordioned between — but several were earthen and a large variety of other species were also represented.

The earthen ones were all classics I was familiar with. *Works of Shakespeare*, a collection of Hemingway, *The Dark Tower* by Stephen King. I could have downloaded any of them easily enough but I was one of those few modern readers who still appreciated the look and feel of actual paper (or even the modern plastic synthetic that was used in these particular earthen copies). My real interest though was in the original guvian manuscripts. I had been collecting alien manuscripts since childhood and I entered the tent with the intention of feeding my long-term addiction.

The bookseller ignored me as studiously as the others had. My cell provided helpful translations of the titles and I eventually settled on two. One was a collection of guvian fiction called *The Freido Mistern Archive* (Freido Mistern being the editor as far as I could tell) and the other *Epochs of Asitot* which I took to be a history. None of the books were marked with price tags but my cell estimated both to be affordable. I carried them to where the shopkeeper stood by a small table.

"How much?" I asked and my cell, in foreign travel mode, translated aloud something that sounded like "*Sola bremin.*" Even though the clerk could hear my cell just fine I repeated the words myself, practicing the guvian. Based on the unpleasant look that crossed the bookseller's face I shouldn't have. I thought maybe I had offended him. It was obvious he had heard but he didn't answer me, instead looking pointedly over my shoulder as though I wasn't there.

"Sola bremin?" I repeated, and his eyes slid to mine briefly.

"Not for sale," he said, or so my cell informed me as his eyes slid away again.

I was surprised by the rude behavior. I had double-checked my cell and it said nothing about avoiding contact or maintaining silence on *bazza* and the shop was definitely open. Maybe they didn't like humans in this area, I thought, wondering if so how would they take Vavaka's new bride? India Phoenix was pretty much a poster child for stereotypical humanity.

I decided to be direct. "I apologize for interrupting your *bazza*. Is it a problem for me to shop here?" The translator spat out guvian I didn't bother to listen to, instead watching the face of the shopkeeper. His *shatia* flickered rapidly once but he stared ahead and refused to acknowledge me.

This got my hackles up. "What is this?" I demanded. "You don't serve humans?" I saw his jaw clench tightly but still he didn't respond. "Well, if you want money for these you'll have to talk to me," I said, holding the books up in his face. "I'm willing to pay for them, you understand. I came here for an honest purchase but I'll take them either way." I waited but other than a slight motion of his head there was still no response. "I'm a guest of Vavaka's. You know where to find me."

He ignored me. Vavaka's name seemed to have no effect. I sighed in exasperation and walked out of the tent, still carrying my "purchases."

I had drawn the attention of several other gobos though they all tried to seem as if they were otherwise occupied. None yelled "thief" and tried to chase me or any such thing. It was kind of creepy in fact, almost like they were zombies of some kind and I was moving through some weird version of *Attack of the Awful Dead* where the dead had weird eyes and weren't attacking.

Though I had seen no sign of it the shopkeeper must have pressed an alarm for a moment later I saw one of the Suburban Military gliders creep into a hovering position near the tent.

"Really?" I said, giving the shopkeeper a frown. "I told you quite clearly I'm not trying to steal anything."

The doors on the side of the glider slid up and two *halikari* stepped out. These looked even more threatening than the ones I had encountered upon our arrival. They wore helmets with reflective surfaces that completely hid their expressions and they were clothed – wrapped, like the others – in what appeared to be some sort of iridescent gray plastic. Also they carried blasters, two-handed rifles of guvian manufacture, which they immediately pointed at me.

I raised my hands (the books still clutched in my right) and said, "I really hope those are set on stun." My cell repeated the guvian translation before I could stop it. "Look, I didn't know it was against the law to shop on *bazza*. My cell says it's fine."

One of them approached me. "Get on your hands and knees," he said. He spoke anglish as though he grew up

105

in my neighborhood. His tone was harsh, threatening. I confess I was cowed. I considered resisting but there seemed no point. Instead I lowered myself to the ground as requested, setting the books beside me.

"I didn't steal the books," I said. "I tried to pay for them. I'm a guest of Vavaka's."

"You are in violation," he said, "of Order 309."

"Excuse me?" I said. "Order 309?" My cell started looking it up but the *halikari* ripped it from my head.

"Order 309-J," he said, emphasizing the letter.

"What?" I said and tried to sit up, tried to look around at him. His hand met my face, hard, and I blinked away stars.

"You are in violation of Order 309-J-236," he said. "Thinking during *bazza*!" He shouted the last from behind me loud enough I jumped. Then he laughed, a long unpleasant sound that blended dark threat with giddy humor.

He was insane, I thought, frightened for my life, but had no real time to dwell on it before his hand – or something – hit my head again and I blacked out.

I dreamed. I always do. A boat – an old one, ancient, some kind of rowboat – carried me through a sea of purple. I did not row. Ahead and behind of me were shadowy figures in robes. I knew they were sad, mourning something, but I know nothing else about them. They rowed endlessly. We floated but when I dipped my hand into the sea instead of being water it turned out it was purple sand, ground very fine. I held up a handful and sifted it through my fingers, watching it drop back into the sea. I watched it drift, trickling down from my hand.

I awoke thinking of an hourglass, with the image of one in my mind. Sand dripping down, a sense that time flowed like these grains, squeezing through one tiny stone after another, others backed up behind awaiting their opportunity. I awoke slowly, over long minutes of an empty dreamy sort of awareness that could have been who knows how long because it happened in a space outside the dimension of time. I viewed it as from above, watching it squeezed through the tiny crux of my awareness one pebble at a time. After a thousand or so of these pebbles drifted by I reattached to the time-stream with a jolting shock that left me gasping, ragged pain searing through my chest.

It was dark but not completely so. A dim light flickered from off to my right. I was on my back, unrestrained. I sat up and looked around. They had put me in a cell, a little room maybe a couple meters wide with three walls and bars for a fourth. I was alone and I heard no sound of activity. I took deep breaths. It was cold but I had broken into a sweat. Something unpleasant slept fitfully in my gut, stirring every time I turned my head.

I tried to remain still.

The cell was not too bad as prisons go. I had a small sink and toilet in the corner which was even equipped with a privacy shade. I even had a desk. Stacked on it were the two books I had selected from the shop. That seemed weird. I had assumed I was getting arrested for stealing them – though of course that didn't make any sense either.

The thing in my gut uncoiled suddenly and I retched. I got to my feet shaking and dripping and struggled to the toilet where my stomach clenched twice more before I heaved up at least two meals. I felt immediately better but still weak. I waved my hand over the sensor, flushing the stink away, then sat on the toilet, sagging against its plastic back. I pressed the button for the privacy shade and it slid into place, blocking out what little light there had been, and I sat in the darkness waiting for my trembling to pass.

I didn't know why I had been taken prisoner. My best assumption was Vavaka – that he had orchestrated it somehow to get me out of the way. But the words – and numbers – of the *halikari* said differently. I had heard the sequence before but not from Vavaka or any in his employ. Instead it was clearly India's kidnapper – the murderer – who had arranged for my arrest.

I again pressed the button for the privacy shade and it lifted back out of the way. I washed my mouth out in the sink – the water tasted like salt – and then stepped over to the bars that enclosed my cell. They were vertical, about ten centimeters apart with thin wires running horizontally every few centimeters. Outside was a hallway that disappeared in either direction. Opposite me, a granite wall. I seemed alone.

I sat on the cot. I thought about opening one of the books but decided against it. I waited.

It was not very long before I heard footsteps in the hall, distant, but they were the only sound in the quiet room. It took a while for them to get to my cell. They stopped just outside and I regarded the man – not a gobo but a human – who had appeared: an intimidating figure, dressed in black leather, tall with large black eyes and long unkempt brown hair. He sneered and smiled at the same time.

"You see, 309. The pieces fall into place."

8

"How?" I demanded. My first thought was "why," but I dismissed it — he was obviously a madman. The voice was unmistakable. I now confronted India's kidnapper in the flesh. "How did you do this? Have you taken over the *halikari*?" I felt a warm flush of adrenaline and carefully erased the scowl that was growing on my face.

"Easy to do so," he said. "They are just people after all. People — human, gobo, it doesn't matter what variety — are easily persuaded." His voice was like oil dripping on flame.

"I find it hard to believe you've corrupted the whole *halikari*," I said.

"Corrupted," he repeated, his tone amused. He smiled through the bars. "You know people as well as I do, don't you?" He smirked like he had a secret. I wanted to punch it off his face but tried to keep my expression empty of emotion. I took two deep breaths, then a third.

"You're a hacker, right?" His smile didn't falter but I judged I had guessed correctly. "You've taken over the police software."

"We're talking about people, not software. But then people are little more than their programming, aren't they?" His smile still never faltered. From down the hall I heard a quiet hum, and a moment later a chair-bot — KROSSTEK written across the bottom — wheeled itself into view. My captor sat in it, taking a second to arrange himself comfortably. I remained seated on the cot, my back straight, not wanting to give him the satisfaction of seeing weakness. I still felt ill but I ignored it. He had my full attention.

"'Hacker' is such an ugly word," he said. A long lock of hair fell over his face, briefly blocking one of his piercing eyes, and he swept it back behind an ear. "It wasn't always so. When the digital world was new those who could manipulate it at their pleasure were often regarded highly."

"I know this," I said shortly. I was a history buff and probably knew human history better than he did. "That was before the Space Machine."

"The Space Machine?" said my captor, laughing. "You think hacking is a *human* sin?"

"You're a terrorist," I said. "Hacking is condemned by *every* civilization."

His smile disappeared but his eyes held mine in a death-grip. "And civilization is condemned by every hacker." I got the sense I had angered him, like I had touched on a sore spot. If he was a member of the Alliance Against Civilization, as his admiration for such men indicated, he was already an enemy of the galaxy. It made sense, but what India Phoenix — or the Phoenix family — had to do with the Alliance I had no idea. It meant little to me, honestly, whether you agreed with the Alliance or not – until you affected the safety of me or mine. I suppose in that way I was no different than most people.

He raised a dramatic finger, a gesture spoiled by its calculated delivery. "You use the word 'terrorist' because such individuals – the villains you imagine – inspire fear. But who can control fear? It is you who feel it – you are responsible for your own emotion. Yes? Or are you trained – indeed programmed – to fear? Have *I* programmed this fear in you?" He waited – finger still held aloft – as though he expected a response but I gave him none. "I have *not*," he said in a way that said he felt absolved of guilt.

"You like it," I said. "You desire fear. You want people to experience it."

"You underestimate me," he said. "It doesn't matter what I *like*. I do this for *you*, not for me. And for India, of course." He added the last almost as an afterthought, his theatrical façade finally softening. The way he said her name made it clear his interest in her wasn't political. He hinted about aspirations with the Alliance Against Civilization but in the end he was just a perverted stalker.

"What have you done with her?"

"I am doing it right now," he said. "As we speak." He waited but when he received no reply he went on. "People want to be programmed. People like their tendencies, their habits. You've said it yourself, have you not? 'All of life is habit.'"

I had said it more than once. I wondered how long he had been watching me, how many of my devices were providing entertainment for the Underground he had to be a part of. "Nobody likes fear," I said.

"It is not my intention to inspire fear, no matter what you think." He looked me over for another minute or so, not saying anything else, then appeared to lose interest. He sighed heavily and stood up from his chair.

"You are not required yet," he said dismissively, "but you will be soon. I meanwhile have some important upgrades I need to install." He walked out and the chair-bot followed. A normal person might have just stayed sitting and wheeled themselves out but normal did not seem like the word to describe my captor. He *looked* normal enough — well, too good-looking and debonair maybe to be normal — but it only took a few minutes of listening to realize he was a maniac. You could hear the crazy dripping from his voice.

Frustrated, feeling defeated, I lay back on the cot, my shoulder-blades digging through the thin mattress all the way through to the metal underneath. I didn't know what the madman wanted out of me but it did seem like he planned on keeping me for a while. I lay there for some time, shifting uncomfortably, looking at everything carefully, considering possibilities for escape.

Nothing occurred to me that didn't seem idle fantasy. My cell had been taken of course so I had no recourse to the illegal laser app or any other legal one. After a certain period I gave up with pointless plotting and grew bored so I picked up one of the books left by the table. Both however were written in guvian and without my cell I could make no sense of the complex, colorful pictographs.

Being who I am I tried anyway, flipping through page

after page, searching for symbols that appeared similar, looking for patterns as though it were a crypto-puzzle. I got nowhere, of course. I didn't even know if the writing went left to right, up or down, or even diagonally cross-wise (as the Lioteks did it). Also, the color-scheming — which was intricate and not merely decoration but a necessary part of the writing — seemed independent of the syntax. It meant nothing to me. It wasn't like any other writing I had ever seen.

We take our cells for granted in these matters. When you're wearing your cell it's nothing to read an intergalactic encyclopedia or chat with a non-terran on a universe-protocol gaming engine. Without it even normal tasks can throw you for a loop and if you're ever without it on a distant planet with no friends, family, or fellow humans you might be reminded how small and insignificant you really are.

It was probably what my captor intended by leaving them — to remind me of my ignorance, my smallness.

I picked one up — the collection of fiction if I remember right — and held it in the air. "Can you read it?" I asked aloud, looking up at the ceiling, peering into the corners of the room. I hadn't seen any cameras but I knew they had to be there. A hacker, a stalker as my kidnapper clearly was would want to see what was going on. He was likely watching this very moment, listening in with concealed microphones. "I'm sure you speak guvian, don't you? You can read this just fine." Of course there was no answer and I set the book back atop the other.

I thought he was indeed watching for a moment later I heard a sound directly above my cot and looked up to see a small panel had opened. A box descended from it held by a robotic clamp. It came down a meter or so and dropped the box — just about directly over my head — then disappeared back into the ceiling. The box was lightweight, about the same size as the book I had just set down, and made of old-fashioned cardboard. I caught it easily — it was much lighter than a book — and set it in my lap.

It was unmarked on the outside. Just a simple brown box. The flaps on the top had been folded across each other to keep it closed. I did not immediately open it.

I considered not opening it at all. At first I set it on the cot beside me and thought about how nice I had had it a week ago, working like a regular stiff at home, enshrined in my safe antique easy chair. Had I considered enough how truly secure it had been, and how comfortable? Sure, parts of life were tiring and other parts dreary and a few bits here and there were downright terrible.

But being trapped here taunted by this madman — unbearable.

Avoiding his game though was getting me nowhere so eventually I opened the box. There was no bomb inside — if the psycho wanted to kill me he would've done it already. Instead there was a device made of plastic. I pulled it out and found it to be goggles. They had an opaque exterior — just black plastic — and a strap on the back to secure them to your head. You couldn't see through them, instead you looked into them and it took me a moment to realize what they were: old 3D goggles, some of the very first virtual reality tech. Though to call it tech would be stretching a point. This particular pair looked newly manufactured but the devices had hardly been used in centuries. In comparison to today's immersive VR they were a mere historical curiosity.

Games, I thought. The silly games madmen play.

But I put them on. What else was there to do? They were not very comfortable. Of course with a cell you barely noticed when you were wearing it. A lot of people never took them off. With these things it felt like dull nails poking into my face. I had to adjust the strap to get to where it felt like it wouldn't fall off but also left enough room for me to breathe through my nose.

Once it was on securely I heard a gentle whirring right next to my ear and the image gradually focused. It took a second and at first the eyes weren't in alignment so they crossed so much I thought I would get a headache. Then it fixed itself and I was looking at a black expanse with a sign hanging in midair that said "Begin."

When I looked at it a little hourglass appeared and started to spin. I kept my eyes locked on it – I knew how these things operated – and a moment later the environment changed and I found myself facing my mad captor. He sat in an easy chair – no robotic thing this time but an old-fashioned recliner – and smiled gently at me. He looked the same as he had when he had stood before me – same clothing even – but the old technology made it less than immersive. He was a little fuzzy, not out of focus, just a low resolution that could never be mistaken for reality. A caption appeared below him at about knee level:

"Dr. Kantsky. –Applied Reality Specialist."

It was nice to finally be able to put a name to a face.

"What's this about?" I asked.

"Please save your questions for the end of the presentation," Dr. Kantsky said pleasantly. "It is a short medical procedure, no more than an hour or so. I believe you will find it very enlightening."

The environment changed again, crossfading into what looked like an operating room. The view through the goggles was from above as though I hung from the ceiling. Though the view panned when I turned my head I was otherwise locked in place. It was more like a 3V video than true virtual reality.

Directly below me lay a woman on an operating table – not just any woman: India Phoenix – nude, apparently unconscious.

"You're a sick man, Kantsky," I said, disturbed more than I cared to admit by the sudden sight of her helpless form.

"This demonstration is for scientific purposes." His voice in my ear confirmed my suspicion that he was listening to me. "It is not for carnal pleasure."

"Sure," I said.

"Watch," he commanded.

I did though I assure you I derived no carnal pleasure from it, just a nauseous feeling in the pit of my stomach. It grew worse when two robot surgeons entered the room. Some robots were designed to simulate the appearance of humanity. These were not those. These were like gadget-monsters on wheels, each with several arm-like extensions ending in things like lasers, razors, and needles. They had no "head" per se – instead on each of the robots one of the extensions ended in a camera shaped like the head of a snake with two optical sensors designed to look like eyes. The serpent-like way the extensions moved made me think the designer had based the design on Medusa or Hydra or some such mythological demon — evil snake-heads attacking from every direction.

Not designed I gathered with sympathy for the patient in mind. One of them had the manufacturer emblazoned on the side, the same I had seen on Kantsky's chair earlier: KROSSTEK. I had never heard of the company but if these were typical examples of their product anyone who worked there needed immediate psychological evaluation.

The larger of the two robots — they were each about the size of a child if you didn't count all the extensions — extended its optical sensor and one of its arms and quickly applied several medical sensor pads to various points on India's body. I counted twelve in total — two I could see ended with longish needles that made me cringe. Throughout the process India didn't stir.

Despite the limitations of the technology it still felt almost like I was there. I felt impotent, the robots right in front of me, but powerless to do anything. It was strange to be in such a semi-immersive experience with the low-resolution visuals and tiny speaker. Unlike modern immersion which hijacked much of the sensory experience beyond just sight here I could feel my hands, my body, outside of the scene still trapped in the hot jail cell.

Through the goggle's tiny speakers I heard a series of rapid irregular beeps, then the second robot approached India and used a large clamp to turn her head to the side, exposing the back of her skull to my view. It hadn't been visible at first but now I was able to see where a large patch of hair had been shaved from the back of her head. As I watched in horror the smaller robot extended an arm and drew a perfect "X" right in the middle of the exposed spot.

"No!" I said as the next extension to appear was a tiny spinning saw. It seemed Kantsky's plan was to perform a lobotomy right in front of me. "What's wrong with you? What the hell are you hoping to accomplish?"

"You will see," his voice came over the speaker. "Just watch."

"No," I said, "just stop! What has she ever done to you?"

"What do you care?" he demanded, and now his voice was no longer pleasant. He had dropped the act, lost the surface cheer, and now I could hear the rage, the petty childishness that no doubt drove all his psychotic actions. "Why pretend she matters to you? You only just met her, and tell me, what did you really think? What did you *honestly* make of India Phoenix, society's darling child just grown up into a woman? Admit it, you thought she was a silly fool, a rich, spoilt princess. But physically what a specimen! So very sexy, am I right?"

I had, it was true, thought all those things. "That doesn't give you the right to screw with her head," I said.

"I don't need anyone's permission," he said coldly. "But I'll make you a deal. You don't want to watch me carve open Miss Phoenix, you don't have to watch. You can experience it yourself instead, how about that? I'd planned to do both of you. If you beg, I'll wait on India and do you first. Would that be better? What do you think?"

Some deal, I thought. It was another one of his games, another attempt at psychological torture. I profiled him as a mental bully, a verbal abuser, a lonely child seeking to force his own psychological anguish on others.

I didn't answer right away. Even with India laid out before me, it took me a moment to process his intention to lobotomize me, myself, I. Besides the preparations of the two monster-bots he had given no real indication what this brain surgery would entail.

But two can play games, I thought. If he could take me to the operating room immediately as he claimed it meant India was somewhere nearby. The worst possible outcome if I agreed to his deal: he succeeded in lobotomizing us both and then what did it matter who went first? But if I were to escape and free India... Yes, escape seemed unlikely, and finding and freeing India even more so, but certainly neither would be accomplished from this jail cell. Transport, however, could provide an opportunity.

So — before I could think too deeply about it — I agreed. "Fine," I said. "Me first. But I want to see her before it happens. I want to know you haven't touched her yet."

India faded out and Kantsky appeared again, closer this time, grinning. "You're in no position to make demands. But I will accommodate you. This time." The image faded but before it did he winked at me.

My hands itched to strangle his wiry neck.

....9....

THE IMAGE REMAINED BLACK. I took off the goggles and a moment later heard the sound of something approaching, a smooth motorized hum and wheels on the tile. A second later a chair-bot appeared in the hall. Not a comfy lounge-bot either but something that looked more like the ones they carried mentally divergent patients around with, the dangerous patients, the kind you couldn't trust to let their hands or their teeth free. It had straps, bars, and chains – the lightweight synthetic rigiplast kind, but still.

The cell door slid open automatically and the chair entered, the bars sliding shut immediately behind it. I wouldn't have had time to get up and run through the door even if I had thought of it, it was timed too precisely just to allow the chair in. After entering the chair-bot stopped in front of me and waited patiently. I set the goggles on top of the books by the cot and inspected the mechanics of the chair a little before sitting in it. It appeared to have retractable restraints, one for each arm and two for each leg, one for the upper leg, one for the lower leg, and a helmet –

protected by slim rigiplast bars – to surround the head.

Not surprisingly it was made by KrossTek. Did Kantsky own KrossTek? It seemed like a good bet. He obviously had money.

If I sat in the chair I sure didn't see how in the hell I was going to get out of it. I worried briefly that I might not be smart enough to outsmart Kantsky but dismissed the idea. Sure it was potentially true but the thought was of no real value in the current situation.

I finally sat in the prison-chair as there seemed to be no way to avoid it. The straps tightened and the helmet lowered as expected. Nothing was particularly uncomfortable about it, there was even a nice plush pad against the back of my head, but a quick pull on the straps showed them to be secure. The barred helmet blocked my vision a little but not so much I couldn't see and I could still turn my head – though not very much – to either side.

As soon as I was strapped in the chair beeped, the cell door opened, and I was wheeled down the hallway. From my perspective the chair wheeled backwards so I couldn't see where we were going, just where we had been. For the first leg of the trip this meant all I got was a view of the receding hallway, which extended maybe three more cells down before ending in a solid undecorated wall. I could also see jail cells to my left and my right, all of which empty and looked similar to the one I had just left.

That a madman like Kantsky had power over such facilities was something to mull over. Had he built this himself? How many people had he kept prisoner here in the past? Or had he somehow taken over an abandoned facility of some sort? But everything looked too clean, too modern, too new for that to make sense.

We ended up in an elevator. I couldn't tell if it went up or down. It was as sterile and undecorated as everything else I had seen. I hazarded a guess that I was being held in some sort of mental hospital. A prison of course, but the sanitary medicalized environment made me think it was an insane asylum or something similar. Maybe we had a situation where the nut had taken over the nuthouse.

Usually such places were crowded with people, sometimes even more than one species. So far I hadn't encountered anybody but Kantsky and the bots, if you counted bots as anybody (which I do for the most part, though civilization was largely still split on the question). But mental divergence often required higher than human care as robots simply weren't up to the cognitive nature of the task and humans were still classified as a third galaxy species. This seemed to me a human facility, not a gobo one — though I'm not sure what exactly made me conclude this — but even so it would have been run by a first galaxy specialist.

It was the design I guess that seemed human. The halls were straight lines, the walls were at nice human ninety degree angles. I wondered if I had been unconscious long enough for Kantsky to have transported me all the way back to the Solar system. It seemed unlikely if not impossible, but why, I wondered, would there be a human mental facility in the Pyramus system?

Most likely it was owned by Kantsky, some facility designed for his own insane purposes. He styled himself a doctor. Maybe he was or had once been a member of the medical profession, though these KrossTek devices didn't seem designed with current civilization standards in mind. If he owned it, it was something he had built off the grid.

I didn't know who I was dealing with but I confess I was intimidated. He obviously had a lot of power and influence to be able to infiltrate both the Phoenix family's security and to control the *halikari*. Hacking was considered the most serious of crimes and he was good enough he had clearly been at it a while. I didn't know how it was possible he had escaped detection. It could be why, I thought, he was hiding out in the Pyramus system, having apparently built a base on Asitot or one of its moons.

When I escaped – if I escaped – I had no idea how I would be able to get us back to Vavaka's estate. I just had to hope he hadn't taken us very far. I had to escape, there was no way I was going to allow myself to be operated on by that madman.

As we descended or ascended in the elevator – which took some time – I had what might seem a rather silly idea. I had been reading recently a lot about the Den-Den. If you've heard of these adorable little aliens it was probably in a cartoon as a child and I promise what you saw had no basis in reality. When I was a kid – when the stuffed toys and cartoons were so popular – nobody knew anything about them because no one had translated any den into anglish yet. None of the stuff from the cartoon is true. Anyway they're shy and don't mix well with the volatile socials but they are one of the few humanoids (if you call being less than a meter tall and covered with fur humanoid) that has demonstrated consistent, controllable telekinetic activity across the species. Of course lots of nucleites are telepathic on some level but the development of prehensile limbs and psychokinetic abilities together is highly unusual. The Den-Den were the only species I knew to have the two in equal measure.

Of course I am no Den-Den, just a human humanoid with the normal human amount of psychic ability (negligible). But the Den-Den occurred to me then and since I had my hands tied I thought I might as well try my mind. I figured with no other available option why not try to psychically influence the situation, try to manipulate reality with the power of my focused will alone? My *den*, the Den-Den called it.

Silly, right? But other nucleites could do it. Other humanoids had done it. And my only other option was to see what Kantsky had in store for me.

So I closed my eyes and tried to gather my *den*.

I had read how the Den-Den regarded what they described as an inner light — this is all translation, of course, so most of the useful stuff probably got lost — but how they had an inner light, and when this inner light shone as brightly as the outer light the two operated on reality in equal measure. Did I possess such an internal light capable of operating on reality like the Den-Den? I didn't know. But I closed my eyes and tried to imagine one. Mine was an overhead light plate, bright white, which I mentally placed on the ceiling, covering the tiny space of the elevator entirely. I tried to imagine it filling the elevator with a harsh light that transcended and overtook the elevator's actual interior light which came from a small grid of light panels along the wall.

I knew based on what I had read of the Den-Den that for this to work I needed to do more than just gather my *den*. I also needed to imagine as clearly as possible the alternative reality I wanted to create. From what I gathered I had to see it in my mind's eye with more clarity than I saw with my *actual* eye. This was not easy for me – I am a bit mentally impaired when it comes to the inner eye. If you walked out with a red shirt on and come back in with a blue one my eyelash wouldn't so much as flicker. My visual memory just isn't that great.

But in the desperation of the moment I made the attempt. When the elevator stopped and I heard the doors open behind me I visualized the simplest thing – really the *only* thing – I could think of.

To my surprise it worked: As the chair-bot exited the elevator, it stopped its backward motion and shut down.

At first I couldn't believe it. I thought for a moment I my imagination had simply gotten the better of me but after I stopped gathering my *den* the chair remained in the elevator, not functioning in any way that I could tell. Whether I had succeeded in crashing its system software – which was my intention – or whether it was just a lucky coincidence is impossible to say. I personally choose to believe that I had learned something important from the Den-Den and while I doubted I would ever be able to replicate such a feat again I believed then my *den* was fully responsible for the failure of the chair's software at that particular moment.

Still I had not entirely solved my predicament. The chair was stopped so I had a moment to think but the helmet cage remained lowered and my limbs were still strapped securely in their places. I tried repeating the trick, imagining the straps becoming loose, but this was apparently too complicated a procedure, too divorced from reality for my *den* to accomplish the change. Instead I worked my wrists physically, trying to squeeze my fists through the loops. It did no good. I was no better off than when I had been locked in the cell, I thought.

I breathed a sigh of frustration and a moment later heard a beep behind my head. This was followed by a click and two more beeps. I realized the chair had powered back on and was rebooting itself.

This allowed me the slimmest of hopes. "Evtree?" I said, a common passcode to bypass an operating system and dive into a machine's central processor. It didn't work so I tried another. "Whizbang?" Still nothing, and I only had another second or so before the OS would kick in. "Contralt!" I said in desperation.

Three beeps sounded and a digital voice announced: "You are accessing the KT-BioSettings Voice Panel. Please say a command. Speak the word 'help' for a list of settings."

"Factory reset," I said.

"Resetting to factory settings," the chair said and a moment later the faceplate rose and my arms and legs were released from their confinement. I jumped out of the chair and rubbed my wrists, restoring a little lost sensation. Now with my hands free and no one watching over me I felt I had truly made some progress.

But I had no idea where I was or where I was headed.

"Power down," I told the chair.

"Save settings?" it asked, and I declined. The chair shut down again. It remained half in, half out of the elevator, blocking it from closing. I left it there. If I was being taken to the same torture chamber – or operating room, if you prefer – as India then I presumed I was already at the right facility and we had now arrived on the correct floor. All that remained was for me to work my way through the halls until I found where Kantsky had taken her.

I idly scratched an itch at my hairline, thinking. Not about where to go next – the hall only led one direction – but about how to prepare myself for the security droids that would no doubt be showing up any minute. Based on what I had seen so far Kantsky had access to plenty of advanced technology. I assumed there were cameras and other sensors and I could only hope he hadn't been watching my entire ride in captivity. If so he'd already seen my escape. But even if he hadn't there was no way I could hide from today's digital security. There could be heat sensors, pressure tiles, audio alerts, proximity panels, you name it. All I could do was move quickly and try not to trigger any automatic defense mechanisms that might be in place.

I walked briskly – running could sometimes set off alarms – to the portal at the end of the hall, a twisted circular thing that looked more like an airlock than a doorway. It didn't open on my approach and the keypad with optical scanner on the wall indicated it was some kind of security door. My laser app would have come in handy right then but the bastard had taken my cell. I brushed away a lock of hair scratching at my brow and considered my next move.

The security door, I thought, had to be keyed to the chair or it wouldn't have been able to get through with me in it. In fact the entire route was probably programmed into the chair — unless of course it had been operated remotely. I figured it hadn't or Kantsky would already know I'd escaped. It had been foolish of me, I realized in retrospect, to shut the chair down in the first place. I returned to it, again walking briskly but with care, and touched a spot I had seen on its back, a small discolored square that seemed like a touch sensor. Nothing happened. I frowned. It seemed the obvious spot for a power button.

I tried another approach. "Power on," I said.

Still nothing.

I tried both at the same time. I touched the sensor square and said, "Power on?" Why it came out sounding like a question the second time is beyond me but it did the job. The chair beeped, the square lit a dim green and after it clicked and beeped some more I again said "Contralt." This time instead of powering it down I asked for and received access to the previous application. I made some minor adjustments to the protocol, sat back in the chair and re-ran the program.

A moment later we were rolling toward the security door, only this time I faced forward. It whizzed open and we went through and to the right. The halls here widened a bit but were still sterile and empty, dotted with security doors but undecorated otherwise. The place was some sort of fortress of the mad doctor medical variety. According to what the chair AI had told me we would have to go through three more of these security doors before we arrived at our final destination – Medical Bay 4A, Neurosurgery.

We passed through door number 1 and everything looked much the same but after door number 2 the environment lost a little of the claustrophobic security vibe and opened up a little. Now instead of just the plain walls the hallways were lined with rows of benches – hard, uncomfortable ones – down one wall and pictures hung along the other and the doors which appeared between them were not security doors but the old-fashioned variety with handles. It was still empty but now it seemed more like a hospital and less like a high security prison.

We continued to the end of this hall and through the security door at the end. I tensed. Even had I not familiarized myself with the chair's programmed route I still would have known we were getting close. Now instead of a hallway we rolled into large open area. This, I thought, looked like a real medical lab and though there were no people there was quite a bit of motion. A large desk-like unit separated into several sections dominated the center of the room and at each station some sort of robotic contraption went about its mysterious operation. Wheeled table-bots maneuvered carefully around other stations that dotted the walls, passing equipment from bot to bot. My chair slid through seamlessly, passing close enough to the tables I could have reached out and grabbed any of the devices on it. All of them looked dangerous so I didn't.

We approached a door in the far corner, not a security door but one with a handle. It opened automatically, swinging inward, and I doubted any human hand had touched the handle in some time. I could see inside the room before we entered and I had only a brief moment to process my disappointment. I had been hoping to find India but the cot inside the room was unoccupied and the two surgical bots beside it waited expectantly.

This operating room was intended solely for me.

I did not wait to find out what the surgeons intended. I jumped out of the chair – having earlier disabled the restraints, of course – and stepped back away from the room as the chair-bot continued to enter. I only had a few seconds, I figured, before the bots would react to the chair being empty and I used it to pull the door closed and put a little distance between us.

I maneuvered through the moving machinery to another door, similar to the one I had been taken to, and turned the handle. It opened easily and the room inside looked much like the other only empty – just a cot, no patient, no bots. Only one other door connected to the lab but I had to cross the entirety of the large room to get to it. I was beginning to think it was all a wasted effort and India was being held at another facility.

I danced my way through the dangerous-looking devices anyway but had only gotten halfway through when an alarm sounded and most of the bots stopped moving. I hesitated briefly but when nothing immediately came for me I continued to the door. When I got there the handle stubbornly resisted my efforts to turn it. Unlike the other, this door was locked.

I stepped back to consider my options but it turned out I had no time for options.

"Do not move or you will be annihilated."

I turned my head enough to see a weapon-laden security droid, the band of red light that served as its visual sensor oscillating with menace. Or maybe the menace was just implied by the large three-barreled laser gun that it had pointed at my head.

"You will enter Medical Bay 4A or you will be annihilated," it instructed, or threatened if you went by digital tone of voice.

"What's medical bay 4A?" I asked, feigning ignorance. "Isn't it this one?" I wiggled at the door handle, a small part of me expecting immediate annihilation.

The bot didn't answer but one of his barrels started to glow red and I heard a high-pitched humming. "Okay, okay," I said, taking my hand from the door. I started to move slowly towards 4A, my hands by my ears. Its door opened automatically and inside I could see the surgery bots waiting expectantly. It seemed my only choices were being cut in half by a red laser or lying on that cot and having my head cut open.

I don't know about you but to me it was an easy choice.

Halfway to the door of 4A I burst into a sprint, passing the door and ducking as quickly as I could below the level of one of the table bots. I had the vague hope maybe some of the stuff on the tables and counters was expensive enough that Kanstky wouldn't really want it destroyed just to kill little old me. It was a vain hope. I felt a flash of heat and looked up to see a scorch mark in the wall only millimeters above my head. I huddled down even further but the table bot started to wheel itself toward the security bot and I was left with a difficult choice.

"Enter Medical Bay 4A or you will be annihilated," the bot repeated, an extra layer of distortion adding an even more menacing dynamic. A sizzling sound followed and the laser must have hit the table bot, which wobbled and then stopped abruptly. I slid quickly away from it and crept around the workstations on the other side. The security bot started beeping loudly – an alarm, I gathered – which was very helpful as it helped me track its location while keeping out of sight. As it approached behind me I circled back to the security door that exited the lab. Of course it didn't open, no matter how hard I stared at it and tried to gather my *den*. And believe me I tried.

But there really was no escaping this time. The bot finally came up behind me and I raised my hands in defeat. I surrendered too late. One of the barrels on his phaser glowed blue. A moment later I felt a searing pain in my chest.

I collapsed with barely enough time to regret the decisions that led to my death.

I wasn't dead, as you may have gathered. The laser was set to stun and I would later discover I had merely been knocked unconscious. As awareness faded my eyes locked on the security bot – the murder bot – and I experienced a strange sensation. I could see the bot clearly enough but the rest of the scene didn't seem quite right. Something happened to my peripheral vision where objects began to lose their clarity and become indistinct but in this case they weren't so much blurry as breaking apart, the pieces flying outward,

leaving only blackness behind.
And then I was dreaming.

····10····

I DREAMED WORMS CRAWLED INTO MY EARS and ate my brain.

Horrifying, right? In my dream though it was oddly comforting as the more they ate the more I could feel my worries falling away like deadweight. India Phoenix? What did she matter? I saw her briefly as a passing butterfly. I stressed out momentarily when Kantsky appeared behind her as a gigantic evil wasp and then both disappeared as a thick slow-crawling worm — more like a caterpillar really — ate that portion of my membrane that was concerned with such things.

Lewis also appeared, his face attached to the body of a fat baboon. He scowled at me and yelled something indecipherable but then he too disappeared into purple smoke and peace washed over me like a warm breeze. A few other people appeared too and they all seemed very agitated but the worms continued to eat away and I simply did not care.

Then in the dream I began wondering about the worms, where they had come from, why they were so hungry and other such things. So I worked my way through the laboratory to the table and found Kantsky holding a jar of the worms and inside they were reproducing at an incredible rate. A robotic arm plucked one out and brought it close to my eye where I could see it more clearly.

I was not at all frightened, just curious. I reached out and it crawled onto my hand. It was about the length of my index finger but not as thick and covered with fine hairs that tickled the skin. A repeating pattern moved on its back, white diamonds on a black background with a blue border on each side. It moved along my hand, onto my wrist, expanding and contracting hypnotically.

Then instead of it being in my hand I was suddenly holding my own brain and it was crawling atop it, eating, eating, eating away. A good portion of the left frontal lobe had already disappeared like a muffin that someone had taken a bite out of.

Goodbye worries, I thought, watching the caterpillar expand, contract.

I smiled happily as another worm burst through the surface right around the area of the left temple. A sign appeared with an arrow pointing to it — "Arena Broca" it helpfully informed me then burst into a meaningless gray cloud. I noticed something printed in the tiniest of typefaces and I brought my hand closer to my face so I could make it out. It blurred as it got closer and I had to blink three times to clear my eyes. Even then I had difficulty deciphering it as the caterpillar wriggled and squirmed. I could see it was a sequence of digits.

I finally was able to work out the first three: 309. Then I awoke.

I'd really rather I hadn't. The hungry caterpillar was far more pleasant to look at than what confronted me now – the leering face of Dr. Kantsky. In my dream he had appeared as a giant wasp. I could see what had given me that impression. His eyes were too big for the narrow triangle that made up his face and the unruly strands of hair that poked out around his ears looked like antenna. The striped pattern of the black leather he wore completed the effect. With the sight of his face all my worry – or fear, I should say – returned in a flash.

"Subject is conscious," a flat voice intoned and an irritated ripple furrowed across Kantsky's brow. "Increased beta activity detected."

"Yes, he's awake. I see that," he said, never turning to face the bot that had provided the information, instead keeping his eyes locked on my own. "Mute further neural activity updates. Alert on vital warnings only."

I thought about jabbing him with an irritating comment like, "Subject is contemplating escape and revenge," but decided against sharing. Instead I kept my mouth shut and closed my eyes, preferring darkness to the manic blackness of his stare. With my eyes closed my ears took over, feeling out the space in the room, the quiet repeating beep in the corner, the close sound of Kantsky's breathing. I could feel its light breeze on my face and had to refrain from turning away.

"Open his eyes," Kanstky commanded a moment later and I felt a light tickle at my eyelids as my eyes opened on their own. I tried a few times but found I could no longer close them. Kantsky smiled into them, angling his face so it was in alignment with mine, coming close enough our noses almost touched. "You can't avoid me, 309," he said. "You can try but it is no longer possible.

You are now and will always be under my full and complete control. Do you understand?"

"Yes," I said. It was not what I intended to say.

"I see you *do* understand," he said, his eyes wide, his nose bobbing up and down a couple times enthusiastically. The look he cultivated was refined, cultured, but the mask didn't hide his madness.

He had somehow taken control over my body, I found, keeping it paralyzed. I tried to move, to speak, to object, to scream, to punch him in the face. I could feel my limbs as they lay flat against my side, my sensations were uninhibited. I simply couldn't move them, no matter how hard I tried, despite the lack of any type of bind or restraint. Maybe he had me hypnotized, I thought, or under some kind of physical inhibitor.

"Now you will simply lie here," he said, "as I perform the necessary operations on your neural hardware. I promise you will feel no pain – I have disengaged these centers – but you will still likely feel many strange sensations as the surgery progresses. Have no fear. Dr. Kantsky is here."

He said the last in an exaggerated hero voice and against all my best efforts I laughed at this feeble joke. Kantsky smiled benignly. Then he disappeared from my field of view. Music started playing in the background – some tinkly piano piece – and a surgical bot moved briefly through my field of view, two red lights at the end of one tentacle-like extension and what I took to be a cutting laser at the end of another. I could neither close my eyes nor follow their path with my gaze, just wait as they passed across the canvas of my personal hell.

I felt something move along the top of my head, a light pressure and a quick buzzing sound then cold air against my now bald scalp. I heard Kantsky somewhere above my head humming along with the music then that sound was joined by another hum which I took to be the laser powering up.

As he had promised I felt no pain but I knew the moment the laser sliced through my skin. It was just the barest tickle but I could feel its precise path, the shape it opened — a triangle — and I could feel just as well the hard edge of the blade that was next placed against my skull. I felt the vibration as it started to spin and heard the sickening high whine of it as it encountered the resistance of bone.

I heard Kantsky humming, humming, and then a quick snippet of lyric: "but they're the only friends I've known, ba-da-da-dum, ba-da-da-dum."

I stared straight ahead at the white ceiling, the pale amorphous box of light that hung directly above me. I tried to shut my mind off like my body, to get lost in that empty expanse of white. Oh, caterpillar that eats away my fears, where have you gone? There was no hope. There was simply no hope left, of any kind.

These are the only friends I've known:

Charles. Always there for me. Okay with my flaws, doesn't harp on my shortcomings. Knows almost all of them though I tried to hide them.

Shondra. Have I not mentioned her? She has nothing to do with these events except here she was in my mind as I lay helpless at my darkest hour. We hadn't talked in months. Why? I don't know. Time. Time gets the best of us. And I'm not the best of us – I had never been more sure of this then that moment on Kantsky's table.

Paul, another unrelated friend, I would have said he was barely a pal. A freelance co-worker, just that, but here he was as I relived some of those casual conversations that had turned cosmic at the turn of a phrase. One of those people you underestimated on sight – he seemed a simple guy – but when you got to know him long enough you realized he was full of so many deep insights. I only now realized he had been giving me advice like big brother to little brother – useless advice now that echoed in my mind like the sound of so many lost causes and the silent applause that heralded their failures.

Michelle. She was really Charles' friend but she was a badass and I missed her then. I missed her almost as much as I missed Charles and Shondra and my mother. If I got out of this – *when* I got out, I corrected myself – I would have to call Michelle, see how she was doing.

I would have cried but I guess I couldn't. I stared straight ahead, cheeks dry, eyes on the ceiling and felt a prickling in the area of the hole that had just been cut through my skull.

Kantsky's voice above my head was full of disturbing glee. "Almost in there," he said. And he sang it as though it were part of the song: "Almost in, ba-dum-dum-dum, we are nearly there."

I heard then a whisper in my right ear. "Help us, 309."

Kantsky continued to sing, his voice never changing, as another whisper joined the first, this one from my left ear. "Please help, 309! 497 has become unstable!"

Several beeps sounded from one of Kantsky's machines. "Perfect," he said. "We have saturated the cerebral cortex."

At the sound of the word "saturated" a shade of pink crept into my vision like soft liquid blurs on the edge of my field of view. I tried to blink it away but my eyelids failed to perform this reflexive measure. Seconds later the pink crept away on its own but then the voice spoke up again, somewhere between being in my head or maybe located in my inner ear.

"309, please, will you help us?" It was like a tickle on my eardrum, louder than a thought, quieter than a sound.

I had no idea what was going on. But I wanted to say "yes" in any case. What other choice did I have? I couldn't, though. I was still paralyzed.

"Thank you, 309!" said the whisper in my right ear and I felt rather than heard its sense of desperate hope. "We can decipher your thoughts, 309. You must not move until the right moment is precisely upon us."

The use of the number 309 bothered me. It was too Kantsky. The strange voices gave me a stirring of hope but at the same time I felt a sense of disquiet, a paranoid suspicion Kantsky was playing a trick on me. Either that or the voices were just an auditory hallucination triggered by whatever operation Kantsky was performing on my brain.

"We are 100% real by all physical measures. We are nano-molecules designed by 497 to assist in the transplant of the obrut but we are capable of more. Much more!" A certain childlike quality to the voices added to my disquiet.

I assumed 497 to be Kantsky, of course, and the nano-molecules immediately confirmed it. "Yes, he is 497W911. His control loop has become distorted and he endangers the entire system."

Now there were several questions I could have asked at this point and a few of them ran through my head, none of which made much sense. What, for instance, was an obrut? How potentially dangerous was the unstable control loop of a mad hacker? And what was wrong with simple names like Gregory and Kantsky that these weird serial numbers had to come into play?

"There is no time!" responded the nano-molecules to these unspoken queries. "We release control to your central neural unit. Act now!"

There was a tremendous sense of urgency behind these words – in fact, they now appeared even visually in my mind as well as on the inner ear – but I still didn't react immediately. I'm only human after all and it took me more than a moment to process what I had just been told. However as soon as my eyes flicked upward, instinctively trying to get a glimpse of my torturer, I realized I had indeed been released from my paralysis. This did not, though, make me forget that my scalp lay open and my skull had a hole in it, which cost me a second more or two as I considered how to handle this.

All this gave the nano-molecules enough time to repeat "Act now!" twice more – the second one looked like this: "@CT N0W" – and I thought all the yelling in my head showed a tremendous lack of understanding of human psychology as all it served to do was set me on a pretty dangerous edge considering the circumstances.

But when I did move I moved quickly. Keeping my head as still as possible I reached up with both hands and grabbed whatever it was that was messing with my brain. It turned out to be Kantsky's hand, which surprised me a little. I had expected a surgical bot. I held on tightly anyway, crushing his fingers with my right hand and grabbing on tightly to his wrist with my left.

During this the nano-bots answered my greatest fear: "Worry not! We have created a barrier to protect your central neural unit. @ct! Act N0W! We will help you!" In my head appeared the image of my skull being reformed, each fragment stitched precisely back into place.

Kantsky reacted quickly, fighting my control, but my two hands overpowered his one and I was able to keep my grip tight as I spun off the table even when I felt a burning pain in my hand. I saw immediately he had a blade in his free hand and he attempted another slice at my arm. I yanked hard and he ended up slashing through his own jacket, yelping in pain. We wrestled for a second or two, his long, thin surgeon's blade between us.

"Hold him, 309," the nano-molecules said. "We will operate the NSD12v2." The machine behind Kantsky — a shiny, reflective globe with two tentacle arms and three tripod-like legs — came to life, wrapping one tentacle around his neck and reaching for his arm with another that sported a powerful-looking vise at the end. The look of shock on Kantsky's face was enough to make me smile. He let go of me and dropped the scalpel, grabbing the tentacle arm with both hands.

"What have you done?" he demanded, and started to say something else before he was choked to silence.

"You must run!" the voices in my ear said with their typical urgency. "We will quarantine 497 from the system."

"What does that mean?" I said aloud. Maybe they could decipher my thoughts but I liked clarity in my communications. "Are you going to imprison him? Or kill him?" Kantsky's brows came down in a puzzled scowl. "I hope they do kill you," I said to him, and by the redness of his face it looked like they were going to strangle him to death.

"497 will be quarantined and restored to balance. You must run!"

What I really wanted to do was pick up the scalpel Kantsky had dropped and slit his throat but I think the nano-molecules must have taken control of me at that moment because instead I turned and ran. Normally I would have needed to take a moment to orient myself – I had no idea where I was – but in this case I seemed to know everything I needed right away. It was obvious the nano-molecules had control as I maneuvered deftly through my unfamiliar surroundings, taking note of what I saw more than making decisions about where to go. I was in an operating room similar to the one I had been taken to initially but larger. Here there were multiple operating tables – four in fact – but the other three were empty.

The tinkly piano music still played in the background. I thought briefly how it jarred with the violent, frenetic scene unfolding. Immediately it changed to my favorite punk-trance tune, an aggressive track I realized immediately had already been playing in the back of my mind and I felt a paranoid disquiet as I realized how deeply I had been violated, mind and body. The music seemed to be playing from every corner of the room — speakers must have been hidden throughout the walls — and it followed me through the door. The lyrics to the song certainly fit how I felt — "You can't make me take it." I found myself singing along. "Try to put it in and I will break it." The fact I couldn't tell if I was singing along because I *chose* to or because I merely thought about doing it and the nano-molecules made it happen made it even creepier. I would have shivered had I been in control of myself.

"We mean you no harm!" the nano-molecules informed me. "We have decoded your worry. We attempt to reassure you. **We @re yθur fr!ends!**"

I was not, needless to say, reassured.

Outside the operating room was a small area with three elevators and a window. It was the first look I had at the outside universe since I had been captured but I didn't stop to admire the view. I didn't recognize what I was looking at but the bulk of it was the kind of bright star-field that indicated we were in deep space with a metal contraption off to the side that was probably a portion of a space station.

The elevator on the right opened on its own. Inside was a chair-bot, not the torture kind I had been offered so far but a comfy, plush thing that simply couldn't have been KrossTek.

I sat in it and at the same time the nano-molecules said, "S!t!" as though I had a choice in the matter. The elevator doors closed and I watched the digital display as it started to move. This elevator looked more like the ones I was used to with a touch panel, a 3V display, and a digital map. I touched the panel with two fingers, zooming the map out until I could get a sense of our location. Best I could make out we were ascending through the center of some sort of tower. It took only ten or fifteen seconds to arrive at the top.

"Where are we going?" I asked aloud.

"Escape." An image of space appeared in my head, then a yellow planet — pretty sure it was Asitot — and I got the sense we were rushing towards it. "You must communicate the existence of 497. **He !s @ gre@t d@nger!**"

"Yeah, no kidding," I said.

The elevator opened and the chair-bot wheeled ridiculously fast through several short halls causing me to grip the armrests tightly and hold on like a rollercoaster. Then we came out into our final destination and despite my innate paranoia I couldn't help feeling relief. The chair had taken me to what looked like Kantsky's garage. I had a choice of six luxury flyers. Even better, two of them I was familiar with — the Tondai Revelation and the Burling Ace. Lewis had owned each briefly — he had gone through a couple vehicles a year even before the success of his show — and before he had Mike I was one of his regular drivers. Of course all the flyers would be keyed to Kantsky's biometrics but I imagined with the help of my "friends" that would be no problem.

I chose the Revelation — it had a slightly higher top speed — and hopped into the pilot's seat. I didn't have to download my preferred HUD, it was already installed and loaded up for me. Invasive as it was I suppose having nano-molecules in your brain did have its advantages. In the top right of the display the SPS showed a 3D map and the directory name of my location — "Pyramus Substation 4AWM" — a generic address with no accompanying description. But I could fill that in myself: "Mad Doctor's Space Lab." I marked it in my memory for later. I pressed the launch sequence and we were ejected from the airlock.

The Revelation showed only a 45% charge. Probably not quite enough to make it to Asitot — the SPS said I'd get about 90% there unless I took it slow and relied on a few inertia breaks. So I turned instead toward Pyramus, Asitot's moon. I knew no one on Pyramus, and the moon was not politically affiliated with Asitot. In fact, as I had tried briefly to explain to India at our first meeting, the two were practically enemies, diametrically opposed religiously and philosophically the last twenty years. I knew almost nothing about Pyramus, but I assumed as the victim of an intergalactic crime I would be able to seek assistance with behavior enforcement. With that in mind, I pressed the comm button on the display and pulled up the local directory. It was only as I was clicking on the nearest Pyramus docking station that I realized the display was in guvian. Again, an advantage to having a brain full of nano-molecules. The translation was seamless — I might as well have been reading anglish. The normal cell interface, useful as it was, paled in comparison.

I dialed and waited for two or three seconds as the display said "CONNECTING…"

Then a voice came over the comm, flooding me with relief: "Pyramus Docking, we have received your location. Standby."

The nano-molecules buzzed in my ear: "You must tell him of 497!" Sure, I thought. I had no doubt they'd do it themselves if I didn't.

"We cannot!" they insisted. "We cannot interfere with the choices of independent units, especially balancing units such as 309."

I would have asked what a balancing unit was but the voice on the comm returned. "We have received your vehicle's identification information. You are operating an unregistered vehicle. State your identity."

I did, including my citizenship status and SN. I tried to immediately follow it with an explanation of my presence, but I was interrupted.

"Standby." So I waited, and a moment later, he said, "We have your records, 309."

At the sound of the number my skin crawled. It was Kantsky — the voice was different but who else would use those digits against me? But the nano-molecules immediately reassured me: the station operator had said my actual name. The nano-molecules had translated it as they were programmed to do, with the digits Kantsky used to identify me in his system.

"Quit calling me that," I mumbled. "It bothers me."

Meanwhile, the station operator went on: "Your conviso has not been authorized for Pyramus. Do not approach unless you can provide an authorized transit identification."

"Help," I said into the comm. "I have been kidnapped."

148

"There is no help for you," the voice on the comm returned, and my breath went out of me like a punch in the gut. It was Kantsky this time — confirmed by the sense of dread I sensed from the nano-molecules. I shivered. My stomach clenched tight as a wave of nausea rushed over me.

"No," I said and I pushed the throttle to full, still pointed in the direction of Pyramus.

"Yes," Kantsky replied. "I have regained control over my devices. As soon as I am in range I will regain control of your body as well."

"Never, 497," I said and heard him laugh. A blip appeared on the radar screen, a small speed craft zipping in behind me. I had no idea how close he had to get to regain influence over the nano-bots — but as soon as I had the thought the nano-molecules fed me all the necessary information.

"497 is 7.2 seconds from control."

No time at all. If only the Revelation had some sort of weaponry. An EMP would be nice, I thought. Something like that might even have disabled the nano-molecules, so Kantsky couldn't take control.

"We are able to self-destruct!" The nano-molecules said — with 3 seconds left. "**GOODBYE, 309!**"

And I felt better. More myself. The change was immediate but not all to the good. Previously I had moved with an assurance not my own, my actions automatic and immediate. I hadn't realized it at the time. Flying the Revelation suddenly took attention, and I lost a few seconds orienting myself as Kantsy closed in. His voice came again over the comm:

"I see you have disabled my control system. Not

enough, 309, not enough." A moment later the display system blanked out, returning the next instant with a red overlay written in guvian that I assumed meant I no longer had control of the vehicle.

Kantsky had hacked the Revelation. Of course. The desperate sense of helplessness I felt at that moment is the reason hackers deserve the death penalty. The flyer turned on its own, reversing course, and I stabbed at the comm button in desperation. "Pyramus Docking, are you there? Pyramus Docking, please respond."

"Pyramus Docking, please respond!" came Kantsky's voice, mocking me. "They can't hear you, 309. It's just you and me. You realize that now, don't you?"

I searched desperately for a solution. Maybe there was some way to disable the flyer? I thought if I could get access to the battery array I could maybe disable the power connection but I didn't know the Revelation well enough to know where the access panel was located. I checked behind the rear passenger seats – a common location – but found nothing save for a charging port. I did find a panel on the side of the cargo hold that probably opened to the engine but I couldn't figure out how to open it. It had a touch panel but it must have been disabled or keyed to Kantsky because when I touched it nothing happened.

I tried then the only thing I could think of – to once again gather my *den* and try to psychically manipulate the environment in the manner of the Den-Den. I imagined a bright overhead panel filling the flyer with my light then pictured the Revelation stopping its flight, powering down like the chair had before, crashing its navigation software.

I thought for a second it might be working. I heard a sudden high-pitched whine in my left ear like the air pressure had changed. But the Revelation continued its flight. I concentrated harder and the whine moved from my left ear to my right ear. The Revelation did not stop.

"Almost there," said Kantsky over the comm. His voice set me over the edge. I changed the vision of my *den*. Now I pictured Kantsky – his leering, arrogant snarl – and imagined his head in my hand as I slowly squeezed, my fist in my vision overly large, huge and powerful, his head a tiny walnut ready to crack. "What are you doing?" said Kantsky and I could hear an edge of fear in his voice. Pain? It must be working, I thought, and squeezed and concentrated, concentrated and squeezed. I imagined the sound of his skull snapping under the pressure. I closed my eyes and allowed myself to enjoy this brief imaginary revenge. "Enough!" Kantsky said.

The display flashed a brief message: "Warning: Cabin Pressure Change. Please attach backup breathing apparatus."

Dammit, I thought. If there was a backup breathing apparatus I had no time to find it. I was seized with sudden vertigo, overcome with dizziness, and passed out. As I did the edges of reality perforated with red static, making me think for a moment my eyes were bleeding.

I didn't dream. It seemed to me that I woke the very next instant but when I did I was no longer in the Revelation. I was instead lying on a robo-cot as it wheeled its way back through the hall. My heart pounded like I had been running and my eyes flickered wildly, trying to make sense of the dots of red that still tickled the edges of my vision. Kantsky walked ahead of the cot, his back to me. I was not restrained, I realized, and he clearly did not know I was conscious.

I hesitated only long enough to gain some control over my state of mind. Then I quickly sat up in the cot, grabbed his throat from behind with both hands and squeezed. He tried to pull away. I stood up and caught one of his legs with my own, knocking us both to the ground. Kantsky was beneath me and I heard his forehead crack against the floor. I couldn't decide if I wanted to strangle him or pound his head against the floor again so I did both. It was maybe the first moment of true savagery in my life and I don't think I was even aware of it. I hated Kantsky so much, so deeply and thoroughly in that moment that I could not stop even after he stopped moving. I choked, I pounded, until I was one hundred percent sure Kantsky was dead.

In my rage I forgot about India completely. I didn't worry about how I was going to find her or how I would get back to Earth. I thought with my bloody hands instead, at least until everything split in half, and I found myself being pulled somehow violently away from myself.

It hurt.

••••11••••

FOR A MOMENT I SAW MYSELF FROM ABOVE like an overhead view in a Galactic Empires game or before when Kantsky had shown me India with the historical stereovision goggles. Then I blinked and suddenly I was looking at the worried face of Charles, close-up, then I blinked again and I was choking Kantsky, my hands clutched around his skinny neck like I was hanging from a safety line. The way things changed every time I blinked reminded me of the gobo eye sim only instead of switching filters I was switching scenes. My next blink I was back with Charles and I knew immediately somehow that that's where I *really* was but it took me nine or ten more blinks and two more camera angles on Kantsky before I stabilized.

Finally: Blink blink blink, Charles Charles Charles.

I wanted to cry in relief.

Charles held me up by the forearms, squeezing hard enough it would probably bruise, repeating my name a few times until he could tell he had my focus.

"I got you," he said. "Don't worry, I got you."

"I killed him," I said. "He's dead."

Charles brow furrowed and he tried to adopt a gentle, soothing look that really didn't fit with his face.

"I don't think you killed anyone," he finally said.

"Kantsky," I said. But I was already doubting it.

"I don't know who this 'Kantsky' is," Charles said, his consoling tone even more awkward than the face, then: "If you mean the kidnapper his name is Erik Boldt. He's a gobo who apparently thinks he's a human and we got him."

This was too much for me to process at that moment – it washed over me like so much sound – and I just looked at Charles without saying anything, just making quiet little blubbering sounds since I happened to be crying. Charles smiled at me, let go of my arms and patted me gently on one shoulder. "We got India too. We found her first and she's fine." He pointed above me and I looked up to where it seemed a thousand slender wires descended from the ceiling. "He had her in one of these too, but he's got a pretty big facility here. It took us a while to find you."

"Were these in my head?" I said, indicating the wires. "Oh my God," I said, "these were in my head?" I reached up to feel the back of my head, expecting to find a terrible flap of skin, the hole in my skull cut by Kantsky. Instead I felt my hair, matted and damp with sweat but otherwise unharmed.

"Not *in* it," he said, "no, no." But he didn't look sure. "They were *attached* to you but when we shut the machine down they fell off. Same as India." He looked at me closely. "You all right, man? Listen, we're gonna get you checked out, okay? Just relax."

"None of it was real," I said. "Kantsky wasn't real?"

154

"No Kantsky," he said. "Forget about Kantsky. This madman Boldt, he's been keeping you in a sim. Can you stand up?" I tried and found I could but my legs were wobbly. I allowed Charles to support me. "Mike and Lewis are waiting outside."

"Lewis?" I said, disbelieving. "Lewis is here?" I had calmed down enough to take in my surroundings. The room we were in was small but it seemed like one of Kantsky's labs. Only he wasn't Kanstky, instead he was Boldt. I had been strapped it appeared to a bench jutting out from the wall and there was a mess of machinery to the side to control the wires attached to my head. It was far less high-tech than the bots I had seen in the virtual world but it had the same mad psychopath written all over it.

Opposite was the only door in the room – a side-slider with a touch panel – currently closed. There were no security bots or cameras, just the small room with the bench and the machine. Charles touched the door panel and it slid open. On the other side I didn't see Lewis or Mike first as I expected, but India, who had apparently been waiting for the door to open.

"Are you all right?" she said immediately, then to Charles, "Is he all right?"

"I'm fine," I said, though I really wasn't, but as she looked more fragile than I felt I reassured her. She was not the same 3V India I was used to. Her face was blotchy like she had been crying, her hair was in tangles, and she was huddled inside a loose gray sack two sizes too big for her.

"I thought he killed you," she said. "I saw it."

Then Lewis pushed her out of the way and I noticed

155

the crowd in the hallway behind her. Besides India and Mike and Lewis, there were a lot of people I didn't know that I took to be human behavior enforcement based on the uniforms as well as India's manager and some of her people. Lewis's camera crew was there too. I noticed there were no gobos present – no Vavaka, no *halikari* – and didn't know what to make of it.

I was tired, too exhausted for a crowd of people. Whether my experiences were real or imagined they had worn me down the same. Lewis, in an incredibly rare moment of empathy, seemed to sense my discomfort and immediately set to work doing what he does best – telling others what to do. In minutes he had us moving, to a transport shuttle I was told. He did a good job of keeping the camera crew out of my face so he must have been truly worried about me.

The shuttle turned out to be a behavior enforcement travel station. Kantsky – or whatever his real name was, I was too tired to remember – was in a separate jailing facility. The rest of us rode in the lobby. We were about two hours from Earth, Charles told me.

"Earth?" I repeated, my confusion evident.

"You were taken off Asitot almost as soon as you left Vavaka's," he told me. I tried to think back.

"From the *pedto*," I said.

He shook his head, frowning. "You made it to the *pedto*? Word is it was before you even got there. From what the *halikari* told us no one at the *pedto* had seen you. You weren't in any of the cell footage or security videos. They figure he took you on the road just after you left Vavaka's estate."

This made absolutely no sense to me. "How?" I asked.

156

"How is that possible?"

Charles shrugged. "We don't know. Maybe he'll explain it once they get him back to the station."

On the other side of the lobby India sat next to Ms. Rhine. Her eyes never left me, her face thoughtful. Not an expression I had come to expect from India Phoenix. Whatever illusions she had about the world before had clearly been shattered. Maybe I thought her shallow, maybe she was naive, but whatever innocence she had had been stolen from her. Boldt — his name occurred to me then — had destroyed whatever India had once been and left something deeper but far more soiled in its place. The oversized cheap dress she wore made her look like a traumatized child. Where had they found that ugly thing and why had they put her in it?

Where was Vavaka, I wondered? If she were mine, wouldn't I be there to take care of her if something like this went down? Wouldn't this be exactly the type of moment love was meant for? But there was no sign of him.

I asked Charles about it.

"I don't know," he said, his eyes shifting over to India and Ms. Rhine. "Something to do with his estate, I gathered. Political, I think."

"Must be important for him not to be here," I said.

"I don't know," he repeated, but the way he said it, the way he hooded his eyes, I thought maybe he did know and this wasn't the place to talk about it.

I sat back and shut up. India stared at me, I stared back, unable to answer whatever question it was that colored her eyes. She had lost her trademark pout. Her face now was pensive, withdrawn. Charles, meanwhile, quietly tried to catch me up as much as he could. After I had left Vavaka's, he had gone online and began searching for India's kidnapper.

"Not easy," he assured me. "I really didn't know where to begin. But since we were talking about a fellow gamer being a possibility, I started with her Galactic Empires profile."

"It's private," I said. "She keeps it unlisted. I looked it up before we went."

"Not completely," he said. "Friends of friends. I sent a message to Claire Cadence, she sent me a list of her top games and profile names." Claire Cadence was a 3V star. I was not aware Charles knew her but he did occasionally move in celebrity circles. "It took a while, but in the end that was what led me to him."

"A while?" I said, fixating on this. "How long have I been out?"

"Eleven days," he said, then gave me a moment to process this.

"Impossible," I said. "There's no way." I tried to think back. How long had it really been since I had "arrived" at the *pedto*? It seemed at best a few days.

Charles shrugged sympathetically. "I don't know, man. It's been eleven days since I saw you. I've never been so worried, bro." He put on a grim smile. "I haven't slept much. When you didn't come back after *bazza* I got pretty aggressive. I've been up day and night trying to find you." He laughed. "I can't say I exactly kept a low profile, like I promised."

We were interrupted by one of the behavior enforcement officers, a polite young kid who practically bowed when he came up to us. "My apologies, sir," he said, "but they want to have a look at you in the med center."

I was about to protest but Charles practically lifted me out of my seat. "Yes. Go get looked at. They already checked out India, hopefully you're both fine."

I followed the officer's freckled neck to a small room where a very small, very kind, very quiet middle-aged woman scanned me from head to toe with a tablet. After swiping a few shapes she patted a pair of dual cells over her eyes and made a more detailed study of my skull, peering into it with the cell's biometric display no doubt giving her all kinds of information. She turned my head a few times, her eyes looking eerily through me. "Everything appears normal," she said, but there was a furrow to her brow that said otherwise.

"What is it?" I demanded immediately. "What are you not saying?"

She blinked the dual cells from her lids and shrugged lightly. "It's nothing," she said. "It's just that you and India Phoenix have remarkably similar neural structures. I just looked at hers and now seeing yours… It's a little unusual."

"What does that mean?"

She looked briefly uncomfortable then smiled and waved her hand like it was nothing. "It's just strange, nothing to be concerned about. Everyone has a divergent pattern, you see. You never see two that are the same. But you and Miss Phoenix are both remarkably similar. That's all. It's a remarkable coincidence."

I went back to the lobby unsatisfied with that explanation. But when Charles asked how it went I said,

"Everything appears normal," and didn't elaborate. Still I couldn't stop thinking about it. For some reason it just wouldn't sit right in my "neural structures."

Lewis also wanted to know how the scan went and after I reassured him, he said, "You could have died."

"Yes," I said. "There were times it even seemed likely."

"Mom wouldn't be happy if I got you killed."

"Well she's not here," I said.

Lewis looked wounded, retreating to sit on the opposite side of the lobby until we returned to Earth.

····12····

IT'S POSSIBLE I WAS BEING CALLOUS. Mom had been dead for only three years and Lewis still was not over it. I don't suppose I was either. I don't suppose we ever really would be, just as I had never gotten over the loss of our father who had died in a shuttle accident when we were both kids. But I didn't blame Lewis for my danger and found the whole idea of blaming anyone but Boldt silly. Leave blame where it properly belonged, I thought, with the villains, with the cruel and sadistic Kantskys of the universe, whatever names they might hide behind.

Back on Earth both Charles and Lewis offered me a place to stay but what I really wanted was to be back by myself at home. I was exhausted and had trouble sleeping in any bed but my own. We made a brief stop at Lewls's to recover the things I had taken to Asitot, which had all been returned from Vavaka's estate a few days ago. The wedding, Charles told me, had been postponed indefinitely so as far as we were concerned the case was closed.

It was likely then that I would not be returning to

Asitot. My investigation of Vavaka was over. I was too tired to feel one way or another about it but I couldn't say I had accomplished much.

I had all kinds of notifications on my cell I didn't bother to open. When I got back to my apartment I went immediately to bed and slept dreamlessly well into the next day. My cell woke me, Lewis on the other end wanting to come over and check on me. I told him not to worry about it, I was fine. He wanted to make me breakfast. It was weird to see Lewis so considerate and it was obvious it was no act. After a few minutes on the cell I realized two things. One: I was still very tired and Lewis – even at his best – was already making me irritable. Two: despite that irritation I was looking forward to his company. After my night of rest I needed something tangible – some*one* tangible – to bring me back to reality, not to mention provide a distraction from the chaotic tumble of recent traumatic memories I was still sorting through. As far as distractions went Lewis was tops.

He arrived shortly thereafter and took over my small kitchen. I tended to go with the automated meals but Lewis had always enjoyed throwing "human" food together and he was good at it. He talked constantly as he always does. He told me what he was making – an eggs Benedict casserole – and how he was making it. He had carried a pile of things in with him, like paprika, ham, hollandaise sauce he had prepared himself. "You have milk, I hope?" Otherwise he could call Mike to bring it by but since I did have it Mike would drive around an hour or two and then come pick him up. He had told Mike I didn't want his company which I thought was awfully rude but also true. He talked about the last eleven days, after making sure I didn't mind. They had released another episode of the show. Wildly popular but he had been too worried sick about me to enjoy it. That was before Charles had cracked the thing open. The whole case was a nightmare, he wished he had never taken it but he was already getting calls for more. Big names, too. But I shouldn't worry, he wasn't going to involve me again. He'd been thinking about that. Awfully selfish of him. Instead he'd rely on Mike for that kind of stuff. He didn't say what kind of stuff but I took it to mean the going places and doing things kind of stuff. It went on like this a while. Eggs Benedict, he assured me, was not to be rushed.

I let him go on, listening for the things I was interested in. How Charles cracked it open. The murderer, Boldt. He talked around these while somehow not telling me anything I didn't know.

My cell went off as he was whisking the sauce and when I saw it was India Phoenix I interrupted him so I could take the call.

"Can you talk?" she said when the video came on. It looked like she was still wearing a nightgown, a silk kimono style thing with a gentle pink pattern. No make-up. I wondered if she had just gotten up. She didn't look like she'd slept as well as I had.

"Lewis is here," I said. "Making me breakfast." No doubt she could see him behind me.

"I'm glad he's taking care of you."

"How are you doing?" I asked her. "Are you okay?"

"I'm so sorry," she said. "Everything he did to you, it was my fault. I can't stop thinking about how he hurt you." She looked haunted and I thought it was weird, her calling me, her worrying about me, when *she* had been the one he was after. Besides India and I hardly knew each other.

But she didn't feel at all like a stranger to me anymore and I could tell she felt the same. Truth was I had no idea what she had experienced and vice versa. Whatever virtual torture Boldt had put her through he had made for her as much as mine had been made for me. We each had been given our own private hell. But whatever he might have done to us as individuals, by threatening us with each other he had tied us together with a unique, indescribable bond.

"It's not your fault," I said, and, "I really should go. Lewis is here."

"Will you come see me?" she said. "Sometime soon?"

"I will," I said though I didn't know why or what I would say when I got there. "Thank you for checking up on me." I really did appreciate it but there was no way I could say anything I was thinking – not coherently anyway – in front of my brother.

I hung up just as Lewis was getting my plate ready, drizzling sauce over the casserole. He handed it to me and waited expectantly for my first bite. The hollandaise sauce was like rich, lemony butter, the eggs and muffins were airy and light, the ham providing a perfect, firm texture to round it out. He truly did have a gift and I told him so.

"Thanks," he said, beaming. "I thought you would like it." Really it had been the perfect gesture. I never cooked for myself. I generally felt that's what the kitchen was for and it made all my meals in a matter of minutes. But if I were being honest there was no comparison between a kitchen-made meal and the one Lewis had just prepared.

After he left I felt good, refreshed. I checked my cell notifications – something I still hadn't gotten around to – and saw India had tried calling me earlier that morning already. I had slept through it. She had called twice, both before 9am. I thought about calling her again but resisted the temptation. We'd already talked and I would go visit later like I told her.

Instead I deleted v-mails, paid bills, cleared out my junk folder and emptied my news feeds without viewing them. I only kept three messages. One was a form from behavior enforcement requesting a written report of my experiences at my own convenience. Another was a job offer reconfiguring a game interface for a neighbor, a single day thing that didn't seem urgent and I might have time for later in the week. The last was from my brother, a link to the latest episode of Lewis Gregory, Private Investigator. I flicked it to the big 3V screen and lay down on the couch to watch it. Kudos to Lewis for not making me start it with him around.

It flashed a warning right away that some content could be disturbing, and it was, as the first portion replayed the initial kidnapping. I grew tense reliving it even though the version in the show was only a short cut of the real thing. It featured action more than dialogue: the appearance of the kidnapper's ship in the viewport, Charles and I with our laser apps burning through the walls, the finding of the dead and unconscious bodies. The cameramen Jack and Jerry made no appearance but I was aware of them in every shot, their unfeigned tension coming through in every angle.

I was disturbed personally most by the replay of the conversation with Boldt on the comm. It was the same voice, the voice of Kantsky in my virtual nightmare, and to hear it again made my skin crawl. I paused it after this, actually stepping outside my apartment to get away from it. I took a walk in the apartment's solarium, letting the sun through the glass warm the chill away before I went back to the room.

The second portion featured Lewis in an interview with Debra Rhine speaking for the Phoenix family. Her comments were as professional and reserved as I would have expected and she assured Lewis he had the full support of the Phoenix family in his search for India and his own brother. Her narrow brown eyes stayed locked on Lewis as though the camera wasn't there, her graying hair pulled back into loose waves to soften the harsh angles of her face. I knew India's father was ill and her mother a recluse so I was not surprised they did not appear on the show. I also knew the family was conservative but mostly kept their politics to themselves. Krumb for instance had sought their endorsement with no success. None of this came up in her interview but these were the things I thought about while watching it.

The last portion of the show was of the most interest to me as it covered events that had happened after I left Vavaka's estate. It had been released before Charles had identified Boldt but did show how he got on the right track. By using India's gaming history and his forceful personality he had been able to acquire all the records — legally, thank God — of the games India had played over the last year. It was a long list but his approach had been simple: to create a list of common players/spectators that showed an unusually high interest in India's gaming. Local behavior enforcement had approved the approach and lent their support.

He must have been nice to Jack and Jerry too because they caught almost all his interactions perfectly and it didn't once seem like he was acting. He even narrated his thoughts through portions of it and did Lewis the ultimate favor of acting like it was all his idea, like former basketball star Charles Thomas had no problem doing legwork for a guy like Lewis no matter the danger. He knew how to use fame. He threw out both his and Lewis's name at every opportunity and probably wouldn't have gotten access to the list if he hadn't. Charles is a good friend. I now owed him big time. I particularly appreciated a moving monologue he delivered on how worried he was about my disappearance even though I thought it to be his only bit of overacting.

Behavior enforcement allowed Lewis and Charles to feef about it regularly on Fefe and the public was all over it. The case was a trending topic on no less than three planets. By the end of the episode Lewis and Earth behavior enforcement had narrowed the list down to around ten names which, to protect the case, they did not reveal. No doubt Boldt's had been on it. I would have to ask Charles for the details later.

After the episode I re-opened my news feed but a few minutes later realized I wasn't paying any attention. Headscenes were flying by and I hadn't clicked on any of them. I was restless but bored, tense, and I needed a distraction. So like everyone else at such times I patted on the LashLenses and turned on Galactic Empires.

I probably play less than most people, I guess, but I still play a lot. My Galactic Empires module was pretty much the center of my social hub as I imagined it was with pretty much all of known space. India's decision to marry someone she had only met on the gaming platform wasn't that unusual. At its best the module was a magnificent cultural lubricant and I had on my buddy list more than my share of alien "friends," entities I had played with more than once or twice and enjoyed the interaction. I couldn't see myself romantically involved with one, don't get me wrong, but that was just my own personal make-up. Everyone, human or alien, is different.

But when I turned on the module this time I found I was thinking not of friends but of the Boldts and Kantskys of the world – people who used such things as tools for their own selfish gain. I imagine everyone had a little bit of a stalker in them, found themselves from time to time searching out what games particular people were playing, maybe spectating silently and watching them play from the sidelines, and while this was certainly a little on the creepy side (depending on how deeply it went), it was the hacking, the secret criminal invasion into our lives that was so abhorrent. These people turned a platform meant for people's enjoyment and amusement into something corrupt, untrustworthy, and therefore ultimately frightening.

Here I was turning it on to escape my restless thoughts and instead it only added to them. Was this the goal of evil in the end, to take from us every pleasure, no matter how mundane?

I tried to shake it off. My buddy list had ten active players and I saw Charles was one of them. When I clicked on his profile I saw he was in Cosmic B-Ball but hadn't started a game.

That seemed perfect. I dinged him and he invited me in to his court right away. He had it set to classic standard simulation because that's how he liked to show off best. He was playing as himself — no surprise as his inclusion in the game fed his vanity. I had been forced like all average people to create myself from scratch but I never played as myself anyway. This time I chose the legendary Buster Blell, one of the greatest shooters of all time, which wouldn't help much as I had the play set to "true," but more importantly he was six foot five while I myself was a lowly five seven. (Also I had nearly achieved level ten on his character card which unlocked quite a few "Diamond" extras that I wasn't about to pay real money for in the store.)

When we played real b-ball, which we did very occasionally, I had a slim chance of beating Charles only because with my speed I could take some advantage of his bum knee. Titanium was strong but slowed him down a lot. In the online game where he got to use his All-Star body from years ago I couldn't hope to keep up. After he demolished me a couple times in standard 21, I switched to arcade mode and started lighting it up with Buster's trademark quick release and stole a game. Charles complained about arcade mode but I wanted to go even farther. "You never play with any of the fun mods," I said. "You need to come back to my gym and play BattleBall." BattleBall added weapons and powers to the traditional B-Ball and before we left for Asitot had been eating up too much of my free time.

Charles agreed to try it and we switched over to my gym. I had to wait on him to customize his power set. Meanwhile we talked, which we hadn't done much of during the first few games. I told him some of my experiences in Kantsky's psycho ward. He described how they had found Boldt, who it turned out had been a programmer for Ultra Virtua, the company that created Galactic Empires. Charles had gotten into Ultra Virtua to ask around and found out Boldt had been fired over a year ago for making his own modifications to game code. Before that he had been considered talented but with a reputation for weird.

Boldt's name on the list of India's gaming history combined with his past work as a programmer was enough for behavior enforcement, at Charles' urging, to get a warrant to locate. The next time he logged on they tracked him to an abandoned Earth orbital station that had once been a part of Ultra Virtua's network.

That's where they found him, along with me and India. How he had gotten us back to the solar system was a mystery. Presumably he took us through the Space Machine unregistered but they were still searching video logs to find out how it had been accomplished.

Boldt so far was not talking.

"I've also got something to show you about Vavaka," Charles said mysteriously.

"What?" I said. "Just tell me."

"Paper only," he said. "Information I'm not supposed

to have." He touched his finger to his lips in a hush-hush fashion. "I'll bring it over later," he said. "Unless you want to come by my pad instead."

"Sure," I said, since I hadn't been to see his cat Max in a while. But while he worked on his build I mulled over it, wondering what might be so sensitive he wouldn't want to bring it up inside the game. It made me a little paranoid he thought people might be listening. The game was set – per my request – to private mode. Supposedly that meant no viewers. But maybe he was just being careful given the disclaimer on the game allowed for monitoring by behavior enforcement in some criminal cases.

He finished setting up – he had chosen a juggernaut build, my own set was trickster – and we started a game of 25 or Death. I didn't go for the kill much though, just for baskets, just to keep it a little closer to the original game. Besides I could tell Charles was getting frustrated right from the get-go, since a juggernaut took some experience to use effectively and Charles had never played the mod. I scored thrice – twice with the same mirage power – before Charles was able to get his first bucket, a slam dunk rocket-blasted from half-court. He blocked my three point attempt with the same power but then my invisibility opened up and I was able to steal it back and gave him a little underhanded slice in the ribs just for good measure, not so much for the damage as to reduce his speed a little bit. After that it was full-out assault mode and he had a half-authentic glare when we finished, 25-11 and me still with almost full health.

"Violence doesn't belong in basketball," he said.

"You mean weapons," I argued. "There's always been a *little* violence in basketball."

"You were distracted at the end," he said. "Still are. What got you?"

I shrugged. "Just thinking about the last few days," I said, but it wasn't that. I had never stopped thinking about it, it just wasn't the distraction Charles was talking about. Halfway through the game a notification had caught my eye. Notifications happen all the time. Usually I barely register them but this one had India's name attached. Apparently she had added me as a friend. I had been fiddling with the menu, trying to see what she was up to, hoping Charles wouldn't notice. I left it for later. "Another game?" I said. "I could use it, to take my mind off."

"You mean this stupid BattleBall?" he groaned.

"We can play classic," I said.

"No, it's fine, it's your house. Just let me take a second to change my powers."

I beat him twice more before he called it a day and only then did I go back to my tray to accept India's friend request and check out her profile. Personally I like to keep most of my numbers to myself. Some people let you see everything they do on the module even if they're not your friends. Last game they played, last question they asked Wikiman, last time they logged out of the system (for some people that could be months, even years), last game or add-on they bought and what they paid for it. Maybe I'm weird but I didn't think even my friends needed to know these things. The only thing you could see on my account was my username and my online status was need-to-know.

India was not quite as firewalled but being a celebrity her profile was at least a little limited. To the public it was private but for her friends she had shared a few clips, none very recently, and I could see she was online. I put her on my need to know list so she could see I was available and started to send a message. But I couldn't think of anything to say and as a rule I don't much care for the random emote.

Instead I played a solo game of Floating Dragon – a supercharged martial arts game – against bots and waited to see if she would contact me. I was almost certain she would. I didn't know how I knew this. But it took her only two minutes.

Her message wasn't quite an emote but was equally cryptic: "?"

Instead of replying I exited to my game lounge and invited her in. I was not quite myself but I was pretty close. I was sporting long hair and a beard, a funny style I had recently achieved in a pirate game, but the rest of me came straight from a body scan. Given I hadn't updated it in over a month.

India on the other hand was completely herself – absolutely stunning in just a loose silk shirt and jeans – except for her eyes which still had that haunted look and her body language which lacked her usual flamboyant flair.

"You look good like that," she said. "Hair suits you." I pulled gently at my beard, unable to decide if she was being serious.

"You want to try it?" I said. "As long as you're in my lounge you can try out my styles."

She laughed but it had no humor in it. "I've tried it.

Wasn't my look." She looked like she was about to say something else, then didn't, and we just stood looking at each other for a moment, reading each other's expressions. I assumed she like myself was set for true capture, but it wasn't quite true — the game had a tendency to exaggerate things slightly, expand the dynamics a bit, which gave even the simplest of looks a bit of melodrama. Other than that it was much like looking at the real India. It was only the edges of the game that pixelated, the peripherals, the things you weren't looking at.

"Your pad is cute," she finally said. "Cute" was exactly the right word, since I currently had it set to a Baby Monsters theme with cartoon style furniture and a plush fur rug with a Gobbler face. His toothy grin and buggy eyes followed you around the room. "We don't have to play a game if you don't want to," she said. "I was just hoping I would catch you on here."

"Up to you," I said. She shrugged, smiled like it didn't matter. I urged her to sit on the Baby GhoulWorm couch, a soft blue thing that was incredibly comfortable but very small, made to seat young children.

"I'm a little big for that," she said but I grinned and waved her over to it. I had it set so as she sat down her body shrank down to the size of a child, so when she was sitting she was the perfect size for the couch.

She laughed and I was pleased to see a real sparkle this time. "Come sit with me," she said. "There's plenty of room."

I did, a silly smile on my face, feeling a bit like an actual child as I shrank down to the size of one.

"I call it my Alice couch," I said, and was pleased when

174

she got the reference.

"Alice in Wonderland," she said. "Do you have one that makes you grow big too?"

"I have a chair," I said, "but it's an ugly wooden thing from some forest giant theme. It's not nearly as nice."

"Yes," she said, leaning back into its soft rolls. "I like this. I'm going to get me one of these."

"You can't," I said. "Limited release, special edition from a tournament. You can't even buy it."

"We'll see if I can't," she said, smirking.

"Anyway," I said, "it's the whole reason I went with the Baby Monsters theme, just for the Alice couch."

"I love it," she said. Then I watched the smile fade from her face and her eyes drop to the floor. For just a few seconds she had been the old India again but now it was gone. I felt the lack immediately and wondered how I could have judged her so harshly before. Maybe she had been naïve, self-centered and shallow, but how had I missed the infectious light she carried in that smile? Now thoughts moved across her face like dark shadows in deep waters.

I said, "What's going on with us?" I wasn't even sure what I meant by the question and the quick glance she shot my way was equally confused. She stood up, returning to her normal size, and took a few steps away from me.

"He killed you," she said finally. "I've never seen someone die before."

"Kantsky," I said, and she frowned at me.

"The assistant?" she said.

"Assistant?" I repeated. "In my time with Boldt he called himself Kantsky."

She said, "In mine he was Boldt but he had an assistant named Kantsky. He would tell him what to do… 'Kantsky, re-calibrate the settings. Kantsky, apply the solution. Kantsky, begin the procedure.'" She shivered, her face a mask of revulsion. "But Kantsky never said anything, he just did what he was told."

"Do you want to tell me about it?" I asked. "Everything he did to you?"

She looked unsure for a second, then shook her head. "Not yet."

"Okay," I said. "Let's play a game."

We found something neither of us had ever played before, a puzzle game mixed with a strategic war element that I really thought I would kick India's tail in but it turned out to be the other way around. We took turns drawing cards with land, buildings, roads, armies, things like that, and gradually built up civilizations to attack each other. India not only got lucky with the card draws but she was just a little more aggressive than me and had a knack for anticipating my strategies and breaking them up before completion.

In the end I suffered a very bloody defeat and my entire civilization was annihilated. Surprising.

By then we were both wondering why we had chosen such a violent game but agreed it had emphasized the strategy side before you went in. It wasn't until the first war that you realized how gruesome they had made the environment. Our one game took a little over an hour. Then India had to go.

"Vavaka," she said. "He's online."

I felt a stab in my gut and with a sinking feeling realized it was jealousy. "I'm glad he's taking care of you," I said, trying to mask it. I felt like she could see right through me.

"Yeah," she said. "He's still on Asitot."

I didn't comment on that, though I wanted to. Instead I just said, "I had a good time."

"We've postponed the wedding," she said abruptly. "He wants to make sure I have time to recover."

"Charles told me," I said. "Nothing wrong with a long engagement."

"Come see me," she said. "For real, okay?"

After we disconnected I logged off of Galactic Empires, suddenly depressed. I had enjoyed myself both with Charles and then India but now I felt the other end of that as a crashing wave of weary sadness. It was unlike me. Though a bit on the cynical side I was normally upbeat and didn't let things bother me. I hoped Boldt hadn't done permanent damage to my outlook.

I went back to my news feed and got a jolt when I saw my own face – my name above it – on one of the headscenes. Of course I clicked it but almost everything in it I already knew. India Phoenix and myself kidnapped, nearly murdered, the madman captured – nice clip of Charles there – and suspected to be a member of the Alliance Against Civilization. This was the first I had heard that officially but I knew it was coming. It was most likely true from the way Kantsky had talked but almost every violent criminal was suspected of being a member of the Alliance unless they could prove otherwise. Being a member of the Alliance meant immediate extermination, whereas if your uncivilized behavior was merely a deviation from core civilized values there might be hope of rehabilitation, if not on Earth then on one of the first-galaxy planets that specialized in behavior modification.

The people of Earth didn't really like to acknowledge their status as a third-galaxy system – it really didn't come up much in day to day life – but on third-galaxy systems there was really very little tolerance for deviation, especially when manifested as actual violence. Simulated violence was fine, which always struck me as odd, but hey, I didn't make the rules. First-galaxy planets did. Anderson Gehrzhaur – an earthling – had seen to our acceptance into Galactic Civilization by activating the long dormant Space Machine, but they still thought we were pretty backward, far more so than the fully adapted "first-galaxy" planets as they were commonly called in anglish. We were primitive and still needed a lot of adjustment. To some of them we were viewed as little more than animals.

Boldt was featured in several of the stories with people like Krumb demanding his immediate extermination and asking questions like why should a member of the Alliance even get the benefit of a civilized trial? There was also background on Boldt, but it was just a list of facts empty of the human element. Born on Earth, adopted by a gobo couple as a child and taken back to Asitot. Two years later when the couple disappeared on vacation Boldt ended up being raised in a civilization support center. Gifted programmer, hired by Ultra Virtua at the age of nineteen. A part of the team that spearheaded the latest update which everyone agreed had improved immersion tenfold.

Then fired for taking too much freedom with his code — judged variant but non-malicious so until the kidnapping he had not been flagged as a potential terrorist. He was hardly the only programmer to be let go for being too individualized. Only one of the articles mentioned a suspected identity confusion disorder, which I assumed referred to what Charles had told me, that he thought himself to be a gobo.

Lots of video clips of Boldt. It was my first time seeing him. He didn't look at all like Kantsky. Most of the videos were old and in them he didn't look very dangerous. His expression was usually the same — a little lost but aware of it like he had wandered into an unfamiliar part of a building and was trying to find his way back. He had red hair, a loose uncontrolled mess of it, and large dark freckles over very pale skin. Kantsky had been dark, forbidding, self-assured. I didn't see any of that in Boldt.

Recent video of Boldt — a couple clips, one of him being processed by civilization enforcement, another seemed to be him talking to a lawyer — he looked even worse. Not just lost but like the life had gone out of him, like there was no hope of being found.

I felt a strange war of emotions about it. On the one hand I knew he was Kantsky and my burning hate for Kantsky burned equally for Boldt. But on the other hand to look at Boldt made it difficult, almost impossible to equate him with the madman I remembered killing with my bare hands. Boldt was like a stranger and if all I knew of him was the lost, hopeless face I saw on the 3V screen then I probably would have felt sympathy instead.

I turned off the news, feeling even worse than when I had started it. Again I felt irritable, claustrophobic. Depressed. I had to go somewhere. So I called Charles and told him I was headed over.

····13····

MAX, CHARLES' CAT, PRETENDED HE DIDN'T KNOW ME. But his digital butler — a feature I couldn't afford — greeted me with ominous enthusiasm and said he was quite pleased that I had come by. Greaves as he was called had no image but his voice throughout the house came through as cultured, polite, and also coldly intimidating until you got to know him. He was really one of the best pieces of AI I had ever encountered, and Charles had purchased as an add-on the highly expensive but incredibly cool Legendary Darth Vader pack featuring the original voice of James Earl Jones. I loved Greaves. I wouldn't go so far as to call the butler a friend, but that's only because he refused — chillingly but respectfully — to talk politics with me.

Charles also was happy to see me. "I didn't expect you till maybe tomorrow or the next day," he said. "You don't think you should be getting some rest?" He looked me over critically like he was looking for hidden flaws in my construction.

"Couldn't sit still," I said.

"You're looking a little more yourself," he said after finishing his inspection.

"I don't feel it."

"I could have killed him for what he did to you," he said.

"And what he did to India."

"Sure," he agreed. "And India."

"Well they're probably going to," I said. "Kill him, I mean. The Alliance member talk has already started." Max finally acknowledged my presence, sneaking up behind me and rubbing once along my leg before turning his nose up and returning to the corner. He eyed me through a whisker while pretending to look the other way and I did the same.

"But he is an Alliance member, right?" Charles asked.

I shrugged. "He never said so. But he did express some admiration for the uncivilized."

"There you go."

I frowned. "That doesn't seem right to me, though. Maybe I've got the wrong profile but I just don't see him as a member of some organization. He seems too much like a loner, I guess. I can't make sense of this guy mixing it up with other anarchists, I really can't. Kantsky seems to be his own kind of crazy."

"You mean Boldt," he said.

"Yeah, Boldt." I shrugged. "Whatever."

"I've got something to show you on that," he said. "If you're up for it."

"Why wouldn't I be?"

"Normally I wouldn't even worry about it."

"Then don't," I said. "It's what you were talking about earlier so very cryptically?"

"Well, I've really got two things," he said, "not just the one, but let me show you this first." He waved toward the 3V and it powered on. "Greaves," he said, "can we go offline for this? Full firewall."

"Of course, Mr. Thomas. Should I excuse myself as well?"

"Yes, just for the time being. I'll hit the button when we're through."

"Very good, sir." The disturbing sound of his breathing apparatus faded away. It was up to us then to trust he wasn't listening. I had no reason to question Greaves but hackers really got you thinking twice about things.

"Okay," Charles said, "I've got this new friend in behavior enforcement. He's a fan. Really good guy, just trying to do the right thing. I got him to bend some rules for me, just a little bit, and let me take home a couple things. But I promised him I wouldn't let this stuff go anywhere, okay? That it was just to show you. If it got out anywhere else it would get this guy fired at least."

"Sure, sure," I said.

"This first thing will be public record in less than a week anyway, pretty sure. I just wanted to let you get an opportunity to see it." He stopped and inspected me again. "Only if you want to."

"Charles, just tell me what it is."

Instead, he flicked toward the 3V screen and a video started. Our view was from an overhead camera at about a sixty degree angle, looking down onto the pale forehead of Boldt, gleaming white as it reflected the bright light turned on him back to the camera. He sat at a table in a black, featureless interrogation room, his hands locked into rigiplast cuffs bolted to the table's surface.

"State your name for the record," a voice said, sexless, curt, professional, unforgiving. Despite the perfect anglish I doubted it was human. There was no real way to tell. I just didn't think they'd leave such a sensitive interview in the hands of a human, and to some of the second and third galaxy species anglish was child's play. Some such could read the intricacies of human voice and body language far better than I could ever hope to.

Boldt stirred slightly then mumbled, "Boldt."

"Full name."

He sighed, sinking into his chair. "Erik Daniel Boldt as'Geony." He said the last bit – the first I had heard the guvian name – with extra emphasis, even a bit defiantly, I thought.

"State your biological identification, place of birth, and citizenship status."

Boldt took a second then quietly said, "Guvian. I was born on Earth. I reject citizenship."

There was a significant pause before the next question. "You believe yourself to be biologically guvian, is this correct?"

Boldt rolled his eyes. "Obviously," he said in a dead monotone with almost no spirit.

"You were born guvian?"

"Of course."

Something was bothering me about the whole thing already but it wasn't Boldt's inability to grasp he wasn't a gobo. It was the voice. It wasn't right – it wasn't Kantsky's. I had just listened to the recording of the comm earlier and it didn't seem to me to be the same voice as that of the man in the video. I interrupted the playback.

"That's not Kantsky."

Charles gave me a look like he thought I might be losing it. "There is no Kantsky. It's Boldt."

"I know that," I said. "But his voice on the shuttle when he talked to us on the comm, remember? When he kidnapped us? That's not *his* voice." I pointed at the screen. "You were there."

"Yeah, I was there. And that's him, that's the same guy," he said, but his tone said he wasn't sure. "At least it sounds like the same voice to me. I mean the audio is different, right? From this recording and the comm. But the voice is the same."

"We can check," I said. "I watched it on Lewis Gregory this morning."

He nodded. "Yeah, okay. I can pull it up."

"Not yet," I said. "Let me finish watching this first." I turned my attention back to the 3V screen as Charles un-paused the V. We watched Boldt shift a few times in his chair as he waited for the next question.

"At what point," the off-screen voice asked, "did you become fixated on the human India Phoenix?" Here Boldt looked down at his fists secured to the table, slowly unclosing and closing his hands a few times. "Answer the question," said the voice.

"I don't think I was… fixated," said Boldt. "I don't think fixated is the right… I don't know where you get that idea. I've always thought she was a good actress, that's all there is to it."

"When did you first become aware of the existence of

India Phoenix?"

"I don't know," said Boldt, mild frustration in his tone. "I don't remember. I saw her first movie, *Crash Landing*. I remember her in that. It must have been that."

"She made an impression on you?"

"I guess," Boldt said. "I told you, I thought she was a great actress."

I too had seen *Crash Landing*, when India must have been around twelve years old. The acting was okay but I don't think most people would have called the performance "great." She had played a mute cardackian child found by a human exploration party that crashed on an uncivilized jungle planet. What he called "acting" had been a lot of close-ups on India making intense, worried faces as everyone in the exploration party gradually died around her. The movie had some intense scenes here and there but was mostly a predictable mess and India hadn't had to deliver a single line.

Boldt went on: "I knew who she was already when she did the remake of that Rokel film, the first time she appeared as Audrey Hepburn. I love Hepburn and India did it just right. It was like she was alive again."

This I could agree with. India's talent – and it was impressive – was in how she moved. She could be graceful as a swan or as awkward as a lanky teenager, she could move with the swagger of a queen or mince as bashfully as a scolded child, and she could imitate the movements of just about anyone she saw. That's why she had made such a success bringing back some of the best actresses of the past. The acting might not have been as true and deep as that of the classics but she was able to convince you that you were watching one of the greats, like Boldt had said, as though they were alive again. Her Audrey Hepburn had been such a hit that it had inspired waves of re-makes featuring the "original" actors and in a few short years she had appeared again as Hepburn (twice), as Julia Roberts (three times), as Ingrid Bergman (twice), and also as Bette Davis, Meryl Streep, Candy Pearle, and Alara Ray. Re-skinning actors and actresses as the greats has been a niche thing since last century but I don't think it would be stretching it to say it was India who had made it as big a thing as it was today.

So far what Boldt was saying probably could have been said by most of the men in the solar system. Boldt's obsession — if that's what it was — was hardly unusual. The interviewer asked some more questions about that, establishing his interest in India as a fan, then got to the nitty gritty:

"At what point did you decide to kidnap India Phoenix and keep her in your laboratory?"

Boldt opened his mouth and shut it again. Then he said, "How long are you going to keep me here? I didn't do what you say I did and until you can show proof I did you have no right to keep me like this." He clenched and unclenched his hands again. "I demand a representative of my rights as a member of civilization."

The voice on the other side had no discernible inflection. "You have stated previously you reject citizenship. Do you retract that assertion?"

"You and I both know I can't *reject* it."

"Yet you did."

"I want to. I would if I could. But you and I both know I can't. You showed up at my facility — uninvited, unexpected, trespassing, I might add — and found my machinery and accessed my devices and you came to your conclusions. Do you know how long, how very long, I've worked on those devices? I started work on those before India Phoenix was even *born*. What do you think they have to do with her? I *know* you don't *understand* the devices or you'd know already that what you're accusing me of isn't true. I told you already I did not kidnap India Phoenix or this other person you've referred to and I wouldn't have any reason to. Where is your proof? Until you have it I demand a representative!"

"How did you transport the victims from the Pyramus System to your facility in the Solar System?"

"I didn't. You understand? I did not transport them there or anywhere. I can't tell you how they arrived at my facility — if indeed they were at my facility as you say — or how they traveled from one star system to another if indeed that's what they did. I don't know anything but what you're telling me. The only way I know of to travel from Pyramus to Solar is through the Space Machine, and how would I do that? How would I or anyone else carry someone through the Space Machine unnoticed? Even if I wanted to do it, it couldn't be done. Here I am asking for evidence and instead you're trying to figure out how I achieved the impossible? You all know it's impossible. Maybe you should consider the improbable: that *I did not kidnap Phoenix, Gregory, or anyone else!*"

"Can you explain, Mr. Boldt, your frequent appearances in the online activities of India Phoenix? Do you deny that you sought out her presence in the gaming system Galactic Empires without her knowledge? Did you not access her private account information without her knowledge in violation of all acceptable civilized standards? Justify yourself on these accounts."

Boldt stared down at the table. "Occasionally. I would occasionally try to find Miss Phoenix online." He had grown animated for a bit but now reverted to his initial spiritless self. "I liked to look at her, that's all. I just wanted to look."

I made Charles stop it there though there was more after that. "I might watch the rest later," I said. "But it's not him. That's not the man who kidnapped us. I'm almost sure of it."

"It *has* to be," Charles said. "We found you and India at *his* station. He's already acknowledged that was his hideout. *He* was there. He had you in his possession."

"It's not him," I said. "The voice isn't the same, the way he talks, just, the way he thinks. I can tell. It's not the same voice. I told you already."

"Let's play it back," he said. "The clip from the show and this one." He called back Greaves and had him splice clips together so we could watch one after the other.

Meanwhile I asked him about something else I had wondered during the interview. "He said something about devices he's been working on. Do you know anything about that?"

Charles grinned. "Well there was all *kinds* of stuff we found before we got to you. I imagine he's talking about some of that."

"Stuff?"

"Gadgets. Devices. Robots. What I'm sure he's talking about though was the weirdest thing. It looks like he was trying to build androids or something. We found all these women in a room, but they weren't really women... Just very lifelike. Some were half-finished."

"You're telling me he builds androids that look like people?"

"Almost. They almost look like people but I doubt they'd really pass. Also none of them were working. They were all just sitting there. Like wax statues."

"Wow."

"And did I mention? There was a theme. I recognized some of them... Apparently Boldt has a thing for classic movie actresses going all the way back to the beginning. He had like a Kim Basinger, a Scarlett Johanssen. He was apparently in the middle of an Arbor Thauma."

"Just women?"

"Yeah, just women."

Greaves interrupted to inform us he had completed an arrangement of clips. We watched, but it didn't help much.

"Perhaps I can assist by constructing a sample of similar phonemes?" Greaves reconstructed Boldt's interview to match the text of the recording from the comm. It didn't help. In the end Charles and I disagreed. To me they didn't sound anything the same. To Charles it could easily have been the same person.

"What do you think, Greaves," I asked, for an objective opinion.

"They show a high rate of similarity in physio-acoustic construction," he replied. "80 to 85 percent."

"I told you," said Charles.

"They show very little similarity," Greaves continued, "in inflection, identity generated ideation, and grammatical construction. Five to eleven percent."

"I told you," I said.

He shrugged, and we agreed to disagree.

••••14••••

"**Okay, what about the other thing,**" I said as Charles wiped the videos away. "You said earlier you had two things to show me. Is the other one something else about Boldt?"

"Not Boldt," he said. "Vavaka. I want you to look at this." I followed him into his study, a semi-spherical affair designed after the meditation eggs of the Chirons with curved soft-light walls, an incredibly comfortable pillow stuffed with some magical substance rounding the bottom, three shelves around the top that fit maybe two dozen books. Charles like myself liked to keep his favorites in paper form. He pulled one of the volumes out, what looked like a self-print volume with a paperback cover, plain grey, no design, no text. I flipped it open and saw it to be a spreadsheet, some 300 pages with a list of values.

"What *is* this?" I sat on the pillow and started flipping through it. He sat on the other side of the egg and kicked his feet up. Max followed us in and curled underneath my leg, disappearing into the pillow as they were pretty much the same shade of black.

"That," he said, "is a printout I was able to acquire from Ultra Virtua. It's in two sections. The first section, which is most of it, is a log of India's gaming history."

"It's just numbers," I said. They went on and on without interruption.

"There's an appendix in the back," he said. "That first list is game ID, for instance, that second list is primary modification, but all the actual names are cross-referenced in the last fifty pages or so. You've also got date, log-on time, log-off time, other player count, a couple other things, I can't remember them all, but that's in the appendix too. Look in that first column. You see she's got a lot of 4177 for instance. Look that up in the back and it says Galactic Zookeeper. Apparently she played that a lot."

"Okay," I said, the numbers blurring in front of my eyes. I focused and saw they were sorted by date and log-on time in chronological order. "You don't have an easier way to do this than this?"

"Well none of that information is supposed to be public. That's the way Kirby gave it to me. I'm not about to ask for something better. If it wasn't so sensitive I'd feed it into Greaves and have him re-digitize it."

"Fine," I said. "But I thought you said it was about Vavaka."

"The second section," he said. "Much shorter, maybe 20 pages. That's Vavaka's history." I started flipping but didn't find it right away. "It should be a slim little section right before the appendix."

"Got it," I said. It wasn't titled or identified in any way but there was a blank page after India's list that separated the two portions. I spent a little time looking through some of the numbers and comparing them to the appendix. India played a lot of Galactic Zookeeper, Dance Universe, Cosmic Power, those seemed to be the ones she did most online. She also spent a lot of time solo in Solitaire Design and Candy Wars, which wasn't really a solo game unless you just liked making and tasting candy. The other ones I knew only vaguely. You'd never catch me in Dance Universe.

Vavaka on the other hand apparently did play Dance Universe. A brief scan of his list showed he also played Galactic Zookeeper and Cosmic Power.

"What should I be looking for?" I asked Charles. "You've already done the work. Give it to me."

He chuckled and shook his head. "Just take a few minutes and look through it."

I did. "This is all of it?" I asked. "Vavaka's entire history? Nothing's been left out?"

"No, that's the entire thing. I asked the same question."

"I'm not going to go through every line," I said, "but they all match, right?"

"I can't say I've gone through every line myself, but yes, I'm pretty sure they do."

"You mean to tell me Vavaka as'Tatim has *never*, not *once*, played a Galactic Empires game without India Phoenix."

He waggled his eyebrows. "I haven't found one. Not in that list anyway."

"But this is the official list," I said. "You just told me it's complete, unaltered." I thought for a second. "It's kind of weird, right, seeing exactly what someone is playing? It's kind of like spying on them."

"Some people don't mind it. Lots of people have all this right there on their profile."

"But India doesn't," I said. "And this is no coincidence. There's no *way* this is just a coincidence."

"Maybe they coordinated it," he said.

"India and Vavaka?" I waved the idea away. "There's no way India knows about this."

"You can't tell her," he said.

"I wasn't going to," I said, not sure if it was true. "But why not?"

"Kirby specifically — *specifically* — said he didn't want the Phoenix family to know he's sharing their information."

"Understandable," I said. Kirby must have been a big fan of Charles to be risking sharing it at all. "But this is evidence, right? Evidence Vavaka somehow knew when India was online and what she was doing."

"Yeah, evidence he's a stalker," Charles said.

Yes, that. I put the volume down and stood up, stepping out of Charles' meditation egg to stretch my legs. I paced just outside it, thinking. He let me go round for a few minutes. Then:

"When did *you* first become aware of the existence of India Phoenix?" he asked, his tone of voice mocking the question from Boldt's interview.

I shot him a glance. "What are you talking about?"

He chuckled and Max's head poked up from the pillow. "When did *you* first develop *your* fascination with India Phoenix?"

"I don't know what you mean," I said. "Also that's very insensitive."

195

"Listen," he said, "I've got no problem with it. The more I've gotten to know her the more I like her, you know what I mean?" He grinned a sly grin. "You know what I mean."

"I think I know what you're getting at."

"Yeah, *you* know what I'm getting at," he said. I rolled my eyes. He went on: "But Vavaka, right?"

"She is engaged," I said.

"Yes," he said. "To a stalker. A liar. Who's to say he wasn't in league with Boldt the whole time?"

I gave him a look. "You're pushing it."

"Just saying," he said. "Just saying."

"I'm not going to jump to conclusions just because I don't like the guy."

"I knew it," he said. "You don't like him."

"Which doesn't matter," I said.

"This dossier we've got on him, you got that from the Phoenixes?"

"Yes," I said. "Pretty much all our information on Vavaka comes from Debra Rhine."

"It's accurate?"

"I assume so," I said. But really I had no way of knowing. "It wasn't very detailed."

"No it wasn't," he agreed.

"What I have to decide," I said, "is how much of this I'm going to share with Lewis."

"You're going to tell Lewis?"

"Charles, this is *his* job, not mine. I'm working for him. Assuming I'm still on the case, which I haven't been told I'm not. So it's my professional responsibility to keep him updated."

"Well you know how I feel about Lewis," Charles said.

I did indeed. "I wouldn't tell him until you figure out what's going on."

"I'm going to call him," I said.

Charles shrugged. "I'll wait."

So I rang Lewis. He picked up almost immediately. It looked like he was in transit, leaning back against the plush passenger seat of his Lexory. I assumed Mike to be in the pilot's seat.

"Hey little brother," he said, a joke he enjoyed since I was the older but he was the taller. "I'm on my way to an interview with GNR."

"Big time," I said.

He beamed. "I know, and I've got another with Culture Clash later. They're pretty much saying we brought down a terrorist. I've got Jack and Jerry with me. We're going to do a segment on the news coverage in the next episode."

"They're not listening now, are they?" Of course they were but I wanted him to know what I had to say was sensitive.

He scrunched his eyebrows and dropped his voice. "Nothing's recording at the moment," he said. "What's up?"

I knew my brother too well to believe that. "Charles and I have acquired new information about Vavaka. I need two things. First, can you find out the source of the information we received from the Phoenixes? I want to verify the information we already have."

"Vavaka?" he repeated. "That's on hold. The wedding has been postponed."

"Well, that's the second thing. Un-hold it. Charles and I need to go back to Asitot to finish our investigation."

197

"What?" he said. "I can't do that." I just waited, knowing he would crack under the silence. "You're sure of whatever information you have? This better be good. We're on top of the Earth right now and in the Phoenixes' good graces. You're not going to screw that up are you?"

"No," I said, though I couldn't guarantee it. "Just trust me. I'm pretty sure they'll thank us later."

He sighed. "Mike's going too."

"No," said Charles, listening in.

"Yes," said Lewis, who overheard him. "I'm sending Mike. But I guess I won't send Jerry and Jack, if this is that sensitive."

"Fine," I said.

"You'd better be on to something," he said. "I'll call you back when Mike's worked out the arrangements."

····15····

I LEFT CHARLES AND WENT HOME TO WAIT. I was excited about the prospect of returning to Asitot. I loved travel, especially to other star systems, but there was also something in me this time — an anxiousness bordering on dread — that I recognized immediately as a consequence of Kantsky. I guess some foolish part of me thought the whole thing would happen all over again, that as soon as we got through the Space Machine we would be hijacked, I would be kidnapped, tortured. And maybe not just myself but Charles or Mike, any associated pilots, stewardesses, travel guides. Everyone was in danger. I tried to tell the silly voice in my head to shut up and wondered how long it would take for the feeling to fade. My trip to Asitot had been my fourth journey out of the solar system and I had never felt any sense of dread before.

A while later Lewis came by again. It was a minor miracle, him coming by twice in the same day. Of course I half expected it this time, since I knew he'd be fishing for information and would probably need to try out a few objections to the whole thing.

"You look better," said Mike, who came up with him. "Last time I saw you, you looked like death."

"Thank you, Mike, I'm feeling a lot better. I appreciate the rescue."

"It was nothing. Mostly Charles." He put a beefy hand on my shoulder which he sometimes did when he was mistaking us for buddies. "He was really worried about you. I'm not sure he slept the whole time you were missing. You've got a great friend there, Mr. Lewis, a really great friend."

Lewis moved Mike aside. "Yes of course he is, Mike. We've always been able to count on Charles." He pinned me with his best business face and said, "So I went ahead and got you booked for Asitot. I've been working the whole day to make it happen. I assume you wanted no delay. You'll be on a shuttle to the Space Machine tomorrow afternoon and should be on Asitot the same day."

"Asitot day," Mike clarified. "Not Earth day. They aren't the same."

"That's perfect," I said.

"But..." Lewis said, singing the word for its full note value, "Let me tell you something. I'm not at all sure this is a good idea and I really need you to tell me what you have that prompted this. I don't think you're quite well enough yet for one. You've just come back. You haven't even had time to recover. "

I shook my head. "Not well enough? I'm fine. I'm one hundred percent."

"I don't buy that in the least. There are shadows under your eyes and you can't even look at me straight." That was only because he was wearing his Top Popper and it kept distracting me.

"I'm fine, Lewis. Besides, Mike will be with the whole time, right?" I looked at Mike who nodded with enthusiasm. "I'll have a bodyguard. And Charles is no slouch either in that department."

"Didn't help much last time," Lewis said and Mike's face sharply fell. That was the thing about Lewis, he didn't have much regard for how others would react. He just said what he thought. Honesty is a virtue, right? "I'm half inclined to go myself instead," he said.

That of course was the height of ridiculous and gave away that he was already resigned to the matter. As long as I was committed to going he wasn't going to get in the way. But he still demanded my "secret information" several times before I finally convinced him it was a secret that could be more dangerous the more people who knew it. I had no idea how dangerous it really was since I didn't quite know what Vavaka's game was yet.

"Have you told the Phoenixes anything about this?" I asked.

"No. That's what I'm here to talk about. I really want to let them know you're going back to Asitot. I'll just say you've gone to tie up some loose ends."

"Don't tell them," I said. "You can't let them know I'm going to Asitot. I don't want Vavaka to know. You think India will keep it from him?"

"I don't like that." He frowned at me. "I don't like keeping secrets from my clients."

"Even when those secrets are there to provide their best protection?" I played my trump card. "Just remember we're dealing with hackers here."

He sniffed in irritation but gave it up. "Where am I supposed to say you've gone?"

That was a good question because it was almost certain India at least would notice I was away. While I hoped I might only be gone a few days I couldn't be sure. "Say I'm somewhere recovering from my very trying experiences," I said. "Doesn't matter where. Counseling? Therapy?" Both were safe, civilized choices after a traumatic event. A thought occurred to me. "Have you worked out where we'll be staying? Please tell me you haven't arranged for us to stay at Vavaka's estate again."

He sighed, giving me a wounded look. "I'm not an idiot, you know. Obviously Vavaka's not supposed to know you're coming. You are aware I didn't like idea of staying there the first time but it was the way the Phoenixes requested it. If we're not going to tell the Phoenixes" – he glared – "we might as well do it right."

He flicked an encrypted itinerary to my cell, told me the passkey, then waited while I opened it and looked it over. We would be staying at a hotel that specialized in serving humans, something called Eden's Garden. He had gotten approval from civilization enforcement for us to act under aliases for civilized investigative purposes. "You'll be undercover," he said. "I've attached details."

"Is all this really necessary?" I wondered, but decided in the same instant it probably was a good idea. Civilization authority would have known we were going to Asitot from the Space Machine trip anyway. This way we could avoid having our names appear in the record while still not risking any breach of civilized behavior. There was probably no better way to ensure secrecy and the fact that civilization enforcement approved it meant they were taking Lewis seriously. "Never mind," I interrupted his reply. "You've done good, Lewis." He really had, to get that much done just since we had last talked.

He smiled. "You all should enjoy the trip even while you're working. You've been set up as former college buddies doing a re-union star tour, so your cover is to party, party, party like it's 2099."

The way he said it made it sound more exhausting than fun.

I deflected his demands for more information one more time before getting rid of him then set about preparing for the trip. My background cover story was unnecessarily long and I did not see why I might need to memorize it. I supposedly had graduated cum laude with a degree in musical theology and had been teaching at an Earth colony on Jupiter's moon Io for nine years. It didn't sound like me and I knew very little about Io. Who came up with this stuff? It was probably because I could tinkle a bit on a keytron and Lewis thought I had talent but honestly I could barely name the notes I was playing.

Charles was an athletics coach – a good fit – and Mike supposedly a 3V audio technician. I hope that didn't mean Lewis was still going to try to use Mike to get recordings for his show.

Anyway I put all that away for the trip and decided to relax. I thought about calling Shondra or Paul or Michelle, the friends I had missed so desperately when under the hand of Kantsky. All had sent me messages when they had seen my name on the news. But I felt exhausted just thinking about talking to someone else and ashamed of myself to realize it.

Instead I went for a book but despite there being plenty on the shelves it took me forever to pick one. I finally settled on a classic from the twenties, *The Eye of Set*, because it seemed to have an interesting story but was written in a boring style I could fall asleep to. I didn't realize that's what I was looking for until I found it.

I lay on my flexiform reading couch, which isn't nearly as comfortable as Charles' meditation egg but does the job. It at least keeps me from having to use legs and elbows to prop the book up where I can see it.

I fell asleep in no time. Despite what I had told Lewis I was *not* one hundred percent, not nearly. I was mentally, physically, even spiritually drained. It was difficult to think, and I was too tired to want to.

And I dreamed once again of the happy caterpillars that ate the worries out of my brain like the raisins in an oatmeal cookie. They did not all look the same. They weren't the same color or really the same shape. They were all worms but some were thick, short, long, some with bulbous knots along the form. The colors were bright, vivid, flower-like colors. There was my brain on a China dinner platter — I saw it in the dream and knew it to be my brain, I don't know how — and there were the colorful little crawlers, spilling off the plate and onto a table, and then I realized I had a fork in my hand.

"Eat," one of the caterpillars urged me. "Go ahead

and eat."

I don't think I did but I'm not sure as the dream transitioned somehow and I found myself back on the Alice couch with India in a virtual environment that was not very well done. India looked like a cartoon character, an illustrated version of herself, and her expression — a comic version of her trademark pout — never changed throughout the dream.

We argued about something but I don't remember what. It was either about Vavaka or about the decision to return to Asitot or both.

I woke up knowing I had to go visit her before I left.

I sent her a message first and the speed of her reply made me think she was looking forward to it. I had no idea what to expect. I had seen clips of their mansion on 3V and couldn't imagine what the life was like but her message said I could come in easy enough through the garage on the roof. But what was I flying? Security guarded the airspace pretty tightly.

I told her — an El Vordisimo — and she laughed and asked if I wanted someone to pick me up. The Vordisimo flew just fine, I assured her.

I spent more time getting ready then I should have, making sure I looked just right, didn't smell too bad. It took about twenty minutes to get there. She lived west of Fort Worth in a neighborhood that immediately made my Vordisimo seem out of place.

The mansion was not hard to find. It consisted of the main house, shaped like a large disc with two small semi-circle buildings attached. It was minimalist, grey, with dark slits of windows in three rows that circled the entirety. I saw a landing port on the roof and when I came closer I could make out the small figure of India waving to me.

"You came up to greet me yourself," I said after I parked. "You didn't have to do that."

"I told everyone else to leave us alone," she said. "Mom and Dad would have anyway. They don't want to be bothered. But I don't think Debra likes you coming over."

"Ms. Rhine?" I said and she nodded.

"Doesn't think it looks good I guess, me having people in when I'm recovering. Anyway, should I show you the house? Let me show you the house."

I followed her into a spacious, elegant foyer but had no time to take it in as she whisked me from room to room – probably over forty of them – including studies, libraries, digital libraries, game rooms, music rooms, ballrooms, and some rooms that seemed like they were just for display, with expensive antiques laid out like in a museum. Hardly any of them appeared to be used but all were kept spotlessly clean and I saw several bots working industriously doing whatever they do. I saw no sign of people at all.

I was nervous at first but relaxed as India talked, partly because I could tell by her chatter that if anything she was more nervous than I was.

Eventually we ended up in India's bedroom. It was almost as large as my apartment and way less cluttered. A large poster bed dominated the middle of the room, hung round with white curtains that looked like some kind of special lace. The floor looked like an ashen white wood but the texture was polished glass, and here and there throw rugs had been placed to soften up the appearance. One looked like a fur Ganesh skin — it had a very recognizable silvery striped coloring — and when India saw me looking at it she said, "It's not real. I promise I would never do that."

"Okay," I said.

"I would never even have it there except it was given to me by a Ganesh and I would be cursed if I didn't keep it."

"You don't believe that, do you?" I asked.

"Not really," she said, "but the Ganesh do."

"Why did a Ganesh give you a fake Ganesh skin?"

"Well, he didn't *say* it was fake. I just really *hope* it is."

"Wow," I said.

"People give you things," she said, "when you're famous. It just comes with the territory, you know? Kind of like not having any privacy or having people stalk you online. People give our whole family stuff. Just today I got this," she said, picking up a statuette from a small table by the door. "It's an antique import from the Ica system." I was about to lie and say it was nice, but she saw my expression. "I know, it's hideous."

"Garish is the word I would use," I said. "Who did you get it from?"

"Krumb," she said. "He was trying to talk me into appearing at one of his rallies before we left for Asitot. He sent a sympathy gift when he heard I was back. Of course we're trending so no wonder." I tried to keep my thoughts about Krumb off my face but India looked right through me. "I don't like him either," she said.

"He's fake," I said. "And so obvious about it."

"Some people don't know how to be anything else," and she had a fragile look when she said it that made me realize she was talking about herself.

"You're not fake," I said, though I had certainly thought her so at one time.

"Thank you for saying so," she said. "This," she moved to pick up some kind of heavy stone, "is more to my liking. I think this is my favorite thing I've ever been given." She handed it to me. I took it, expecting it to be heavier than it was. It was some kind of many faceted crystal, each facet a different color, not shiny or sparkling but instead deep, warm blues, greens and oranges that seemed somehow to pull you into their depths. Different shades seemed to move like waters under dark mirrors.

"What is this?" I asked.

"An egg," she said.

"An *egg*?" I repeated, suddenly holding it far more carefully.

"An Antaginuan eon egg. It still has probably a thousand years before hatching and it's indestructible, so don't look so worried."

I handed it back. "You got it from an Antaginuan?"

"No," she said, "but a girl I did a modeling shoot with had a bunch of them. I don't know where she got them but I was little, you know? I never really thought about stuff like that. I just thought it was so beautiful."

"It is."

She set it down and invited to the corner of the room, to a couch she referred to as her "settee," with a little entertainment table in front of it, the kind that served you drinks or projected 3V anywhere in its vicinity. I wondered if a small one like that could reach across this large a room. I'd seen them advertised but there was no way I could afford one. I was happy enough with my single in-wall 3V.

She looked so good. She had on a long blue dress, simple in design, pulled tight around the waist in a retro seventies sort of way. Her long, delicate face glowed, not looking any the worse for wear despite the ordeal of the last weeks, and her eyes were soft green jewels that hardly left mine. She said everything felt off since she had gotten back and told me how relieved she was they had gotten Boldt, and how it all made sense with him being a member of the Alliance Against Civilization, but things still didn't feel right, it's not like anything was back to normal. It didn't *feel* like they had captured him, she said, did I feel like that? I told her of course I didn't and that with the treatment we had undergone at his hands it seemed unlikely we would feel resolved about it any time soon, no matter what happened with Boldt. I told her I was thinking about getting therapy myself, that of course counseling is what was recommended in these situations.

She didn't like the idea of therapy at all. She said, "I'm afraid of what they might ask me. What if instead of fixing me they just make things worse? I never really worried about things like this before. Are they going to make it so I can go back to the way I was? I don't want to think about these things. What if they want me to go even farther, think about it even more, dig stuff out? What if they find out there's even *more* wrong with me, and I didn't even know it. How am I supposed to know if I'm really civilized? Besides, I know the therapist or whoever would take one look at me and decide I was stupid. I can't talk to them if they think I'm stupid."

She seemed like she needed comforting and I moved a little closer on the couch to put my arm around her. A part of me felt bad, like I was taking advantage. "You're not stupid," I said.

"You're only saying that now," she said. She looked away from me. "I think you mean it too. But you didn't think that before."

"Things change," I said.

She turned back to me and I leaned in to kiss her. She seemed to expect it but just before our lips met her digital butler interrupted: "Drinks are prepared." We both pulled away. It had been kind of a thoughtless moment, more body than mind, and we exchanged guilty looks.

But after we had each sipped our cokes and set them down again I decided the hell with it and kissed her again. She didn't expect it this time, and maybe that's why she didn't stop me right away. My tongue teased her lip, my face brushed her face, the scent of her swept any other thought away. Vavaka was gone from my mind, even Kantsky, and for a moment there was nothing but India, India, India.

····**16**····

WE MADE OUT FOR A WHILE, who knows how long really, because it was a timeless experience. When we separated it was like slowly waking up from a dream, the outside world gradually returning. I saw the same in her face, her eyes half-focused then slowly tuning in on me.

"Oh, no," she said and without thinking I reached up to brush her forehead, smooth away the wrinkle of worry that had appeared there. But I could say the same thing. What had I gotten myself into? I knew I was lost. When I fell, I fell hard, and somewhere along the way I had fallen for India Phoenix. With me that meant not a whole lot else mattered.

"Oh, yes," I said. I kissed her again, but it was different, more aware, both of us self-conscious.

"I'm engaged," she said.

"Don't I know it," I said but without attention. All I had was reserved for looking at her in this new light, taking her in as I hadn't allowed myself to before, acknowledging her perfection.

"It's not right," she said and I agreed, but it wasn't

exactly uncivilized either. "Oh, my God, I don't know what's going on."

"I don't want you to marry Vavaka," I said baldly.

"But I love him," she said. That she said it without hesitation pierced through me like a laser.

"Do you?" I said. "How can you?"

"I do," she said but she sounded to me less sure this time, more like she was thinking it over.

"Do you even know him?" I asked but immediately wanted to take it back. I didn't want to question her or to argue with her or for there to be any conflict between us. I also didn't want to tell her what I knew about Vavaka's gaming history. I wanted to know what was going on first. Now I felt guilty about the whole thing, about going to Asitot, about keeping it from her.

"Do I even know you?" she asked and to my dismay started crying. "I don't even know *me*," she sobbed. "I just don't know what's going on."

I didn't either. But I intended to figure it out.

I met up later in the day with Charles and Mike and we went together to the Space Machine. We took one of the public tram ships since we were laying low as normal people instead of under the umbrella of the Phoenixes.

Charles could immediately sense something different about my attitude. He didn't try to get anything out of me with Mike there which means he probably knew exactly what it was. I expected as soon as we got a moment alone he'd tell me what he thought about my thing for India, and I wasn't wrong. When Mike went to get us snacks Charles jumped on it.

"So what happened?" he said. "You go online with India?"

"What do you mean?" I said.

"You're elsewhere, man. Only one thing ever gives you that elsewhere look. You're fiending for somebody and if I know my bodies in this case the other one would have to be India Phoenix."

"I went over to her house this morning," I said.

He looked me over. "You didn't," he said.

"We hung out."

"Should you be complicating things right now? Really, should you?" He patted my arm. "I don't just mean in terms of this case, I'm talking about *you*. Are you sure you're all right, man? You haven't been the same since Boldt. And listen, no one expects you to be. But should you be complicating your life this fast? You two just got back."

"Life is always complicated," I said, which is something I believed even when life was simple.

"I'm not sure if you should have come on this trip," Charles said. "Maybe you should have taken a few days."

I demurred as Mike returned and handed us pizza. Mike led the rest of the idle chatter until we boarded. Mike could come off as the silent type — especially when Lewis was around — but if you let him he could also spin off monologues like nobody's business, the unstressful kind where you only had to half-listen if even that and didn't even really have to acknowledge he was talking. We also spent the time practicing our cover stories, getting used to our fake names (I was now an "Alex," Charles an "Eric," and Mike an "Adam"), etc. We took

213

the pills, shuffled down the hallway and slept through space and time to Asitot.

I dreamed I was riding on a ribbon, a long string typeset with characters moving too fast to make out, but I got the impression they were numbers. I was zipping along, the ribbon like a magic road that allowed me to fly forward. I don't remember anything else but I remember the numbers were supposed to be important. If I could just slow down and make out the numbers I'd learn something crucial.

At the end I saw they weren't numbers, but a word: "abracadabra."

But that wasn't quite right. I was missing something, but what I couldn't remember.

On the other side we took a more traditional route this time, a tourist shuttle to the planet, and rented a guide-car for our stay. The guide-cars were automated. You just told it your destination if you had somewhere specific in mind or it could take you to any of the "recommended" places. It came with a full guide app to download to the cell with the local area covered in commercial, cultural, historical, and geographical detail.

Our hotel was incredibly razz. It turned out Eden's Garden had themed resorts and ours was based on the old classic Intergalactic Warriors movies, one of my favorite franchises. The entire environment replicated to a tee the fictional planet of Beersol, a desert planet similar to Asitot. It was crowded with humans, scarcely a gobo in sight, and the ones I did see invariably worked there. The hotel was above ground whereas most of the city – which I had yet to really visit – was underground. Jebala was a pretty major tourist destination because of its legendary formations and also because on the surface they embraced galactic visitation. A deeper look though showed – as was often the case – it had more to do with tourism as an industry than a truly cosmopolitan culture. Asitot was not resource-heavy and instead had relied on tourism, art and fashion to make up the difference in the galactic marketplace.

We each had our own bedroom connected to a single suite. I claimed mine first then settled in to the suite to pull up the local map on the 3V. We were on the edge of Jebala about 30 kilometers or so from Vavaka's estate, even further south. I called the front desk and asked one of the ladies working there – all humans – if there were any sights worth seeing in that direction.

"Not really," she said. "City's the other way. Most out that direction is privately owned."

"Really?" I asked. "Who owns it?" I was hoping to hear Vavaka's name without having to bring it up but was disappointed.

"Couldn't say," she said. "Upscale area. Probably goes back generations, but I couldn't tell you who owns it."

I thanked her and hung up. I needed to figure out a way to get back to that *pedto* without being noticed by anyone associated with Vavaka. "Back" to the *pedto* I realized even as I thought it wasn't right, of course. I had never actually made it to the *pedto*. Boldt had somehow gotten to me before then.

This made me adamant to begin there. It would wait, I thought, until I knew how to approach it discreetly but

I wanted to see the real thing. How was it different from what Boldt had somehow presented to me?

I called Charles in to brainstorm. Mike came too and I let him listen.

"Did I not tell you?" said Charles. "I've been there already. When you didn't come back we went looking for you."

It occurred to me only then that I hadn't really asked them about their experiences on Asitot, those eleven days I had been missing. I knew not *all* of it had been on Asitot, of course, that they had gone back to the solar system when the trail led to Boldt, but what about before then? It wasn't just the *pedto* either. I had barely gotten to see Vavaka's estate. I reminded them of this and begged for information. The *pedto* they described was not what I had experienced at all. Instead, they had gone underground to a market laid out in a circle, not too different in appearance from Jebala but less crowded. They described an alien but still familiar atmosphere with friendly gobos not terribly used to tourists but quite willing to help out. They had sensed no resistance to civilization and Mike had bought several things at the market.

Vavaka's estate they had seen much more of, but surprisingly little of Vavaka himself.

"Based on his crib," Charles said, "he seems to be a pretty simple guy."

"Hardly seemed lived in," Mike said.

"You talk to any of the staff?" I asked. "There were guards at the gate. What about them?"

"Not really," Charles said. "Most of it was automated." The surface building was only a small part of the estate but it had seemed they both agreed more like a hotel or a museum than a place someone lived.

"But you know how rich people are," Mike said, and I thought about India's house and agreed.

In short they could tell me nothing useful about the gobo himself and only very little about the area. I was not at all surprised most of Vavaka's estate was underground, as was the *pedto*, though I found the detail to be an odd variance from my memory. Why had Boldt presented it above ground instead of as it actually appeared? Was there a reason for the not-so-minor detail? Or just part of his game?

Both Charles and Mike had visited Jebala a couple times, mostly to meet with civilization enforcement, so they had gotten a little used to its underground nature, and they both had a few sights they were hoping to get back to see.

"It's not a bad city," Mike said. "Real big."

"You'd think it would be darker, it being completely underground," Charles added, "but there's a lot of natural lighting and on top of that they've got the electric stuff. They've cultivated these bioluminescent creatures — some kind of algae or something — that grow on the walls and light everything up. It's really amazing, you'll see."

I had indeed seen videos and I was very much looking forward to it. So we made plans for the next day to visit Jebala. I was impatient to get back to the *pedto* and to Vavaka's property but they convinced me to give that a day or two. It was more likely we would be able to find out about Vavaka in the city, Charles said, where it would be a lot easier to talk to people. We wouldn't be the only humans. We'd be far less likely to be noticed. And it would give us time to come up with a reason, given our cover stories, to head out the other way.

So after a quarter turn of sleeping we hopped in the guide car and started on the tour we had selected, a self-paced visit to some of the more popular attractions in the city. The car, of guvian manufacture, functioned equally well in the air or on the ground but was designed specifically for the road-tunnels on Asitot.

What I had told India – a lie I regretted but didn't see how to avoid – was that I was going to therapy and it might take a little time. She had not seemed to think it a bad idea. In fact she had mentioned the possibility for herself. But I had left her with most everything unresolved. How we felt, what we would do, when we would discuss it again. Before we left the hotel, I saw she had sent me two messages. Neither could really be called important though they felt that way to me. One was a short but sweet hope I was doing well and maybe if I was able to let her know how things were going. The other, which I watched three times before saving, was a rambling thing where she appeared half-asleep and was trying to describe a dream she'd just had. It had featured Boldt and myself and she had woken up frightened, thinking of me.

She was on my mind, then, strongly, during the Jebala tour but there was no being distracted – or "elsewhere," as Charles would put it – from the array of sights and sounds we enjoyed. I was fully engaged in taking as much in as I could. How lucky was I to live in a time when mankind could see such sights as these?

Everything is different on another planet. I had seen aboveground and it was interesting enough but honestly Asitot's surface didn't compare to Earth's lush green beauty. Underground on the other hand was a completely different story. First a spectacular array of life had evolved in the caves of Asitot, much of it developed around the bioluminescence Charles had mentioned. Imagine sparkling butterflies and bat-like birds with glowing wings that hunted them. Then gobos had spent thousands of years carving out monstrous caverns deeper and deeper into the ground and their technology had developed accordingly. Unlike Earth's in-your-face tech that had worked its way into every aspect of our lives Asitot still *seemed* largely natural but a lot of it was camouflage, like electric lighting that simulated the phosphorescent algae that grew naturally.

This algae by the way came in a variety of colors, but the prevailing color overall was blue so everything had a rather cool vibe. The roads were tunnels but they frequently had viewports cut through so you could see the city inside — Jebala, a collection of connected caverns larger than anything you could imagine on Earth, a kilometer high at least for the largest one.

Anyway, I could spend all day describing the things I'd never seen before, there was just too much of it. The car informed us it was just about the traditional time for breakfast and asked if we would like to try one of the city's famous eateries. Sure, we said. Recommend by price, location, popularity, or style, the car wanted to know. Could we get a list of styles, please? Of course, but we didn't recognize any of them except two: Earth-

Italian, Earth-Chinese.

"Gobo food is kind of boring anyway," said Mike. "I tried it when we were here last time. It's like sludge."

"Smoothies," said Charles. "Yeah, it's like slime."

"Okay," I said. "Chinese?" We agreed on it and went to a nice place run by an interesting married couple, an Earthen woman of Asian descent who had married a gobo. I chatted with her a bit while I ate my steamed buns, but it was difficult, since she spoke very little anglish, mostly guvian and mandarin. But their marriage gave me an excuse to bring up Vavaka, obliquely:

"I heard another Earthen woman is marrying someone from near here, is that true?"

But she had heard nothing about it. I didn't bring up Vavaka's name, not yet, but I assumed then it was not something that the locals made a big deal of. She recommended our next site, an anonymous painting in the neighborhood – kind of what we would think of as graffiti but here in Jebala and over much of Asitot it was considered a highly respected cultural aesthetic.

Using a guide car, she said, was not necessarily the best way to find such places but she gave us the locations of a few of her favorites.

So we went to visit the "painting" which the locals called The Crooked One. It was impressive. It was located in the upper portion of the city on a ledge near the top of one the caverns. The image was about six meters high and much of the coloring had its own luminescence. I believe it was supposed to be a person but it could have been male or female, gobo or human. A dark red light coiled around it and somehow a crooked line pulsed within the paint, starting at what I think was the right shoulder and going down to what could have been the right foot.

There were two other humans there, a couple of older gentlemen, and Mike had no problem starting up a conversation. They recognized Charles after a few minutes but he said he was just trying to keep a low profile, enjoy a vacation, and they promised to keep his secret. From them we got a recommendation for our next visit, a nearby sparkling pool with a connected aquarium. My contributions to the conversation consisted of leading questions designed to get information about anything, anything at all.

The aquarium was fun but didn't help much with our case. I did enjoy the sparkling pool... Sparkling I guess referred to the clarity of the water and the way the bioluminescent fish glittered through it. I've always thought fish looked alien anyway and almost any of these, were they lit a little less brightly and colorfully, seemed to me could have come from Earth.

The aquarium by the way was not done like an Earth aquarium with each creature in a separate tank. On Asitot they didn't like keeping them captive at all so instead the "aquarium" had been built around a natural pool and the building inside allowed you to view the creatures close-up through the use of 3V cameras.

After the aquarium I asked the guide car about U-Ship. Surely their headquarters were in the area if Vavaka owned the operation.

But the guide came up with nothing. I checked my cell, looking up U-Ship on the wiki. Strangely enough it didn't show up on the Asitot wiki, just the Earth one. U-

Ship outlets appeared all over Earth. It was one of the most popular rental companies for transportation but I was surprised to find they didn't operate on Asitot, or if they did it was under another name. The website didn't list U-Ship's owner, per se, but it did say it was an as'Tatim corporation, and when I followed that link it led to both information about the company and the as'Tatim family with some history I had not previously read. It was an old, established family in the North with Vavaka as'Tatim — who did not have his own biography in the wiki — being the lone survivor to inherit the fortune. His parents, Dolon and Beriav, had died twenty years ago but it didn't say how.

I returned to the U-Ship page and saw the listed address was on Earth — Houston, in fact. Surely the Phoenixes had been aware of his local affiliation and it probably meant nothing. But I thought it strange that the owner of U-Ship would live on Asitot while the company itself was headquartered on Earth unless — and the wiki site didn't make this clear — almost all of its business was Earth-related. I wondered how Vavaka and the as-Tatims had gotten into business on Earth.

I talked it over with Mike and Charles but neither of them had any ideas either. Except Mike wanted to call Lewis.

"He could get those headquarters in Houston checked out," he said.

"Not yet," I said. According to the wiki the location of the as'Tatim corporation was much closer. I pulled it up on the guide console. It looked to be a small building in the western lower portion of town. From the 3V map it appeared to be deep in a series of catacombs, the lower portion being less accessible it seemed than the upper portions throughout the city. According to the guide everything around it seemed like warehouses and office buildings, though the translations were a little wonky. An example: "Facility of Supply Chip Storage de'Rakna corporation." Vavaka's company was listed as "Private Holdings Management as'Tatim corporation" and two others in the area were described the same. Not an area, really, that three traveling Earth partiers would have any reason to visit.

Except looking over the map I did see one place that such a group might be interested, labeled "Imbibable Liquid Fermentation Plant Ashbom corporation." I showed it to Charles.

"What, a brewery?" he said. "That could be fun. Do they do tours?"

I found their website easily; Ashbom it turned out was the opposite of U-Ship. They were proud of what they did, advertised their location, offered a large selection of drinks and were proud to have become one of the first fermentation plants in Asitot's history to locally brew varieties introduced from other planets, including Earth ale. Did they offer tours? Indeed they did. Was an appointment required? Not at all. Free sample tasting included in the tour? Absolutely.

Was the tour free of charge? No. But it was affordable and we all agreed it would be fun.

To get there, the guide car had to drive right in front of the as-Tatim headquarters. It was a small enclosure cut out of the rock of the cavern just like many of the other Jebala dwellings, with a closed gate-like door in front and no signage or identifying markings of any kind. For all we could see it could easily have been empty. There was nothing to indicate it even used electricity, though that didn't mean it didn't since the typical guvian style was to camouflage such things. Anyway its appearance told me nothing useful.

We enjoyed ourselves tremendously at the brewery, which seemed very cosmopolitan despite the fact it didn't seem to do a whole lot of tours. They seemed a little surprised when we showed up without notice but were very happy to see us. The clerk who greeted us spoke anglish decently and was quick working with his translator app when he struggled so we had no trouble communicating.

Like the as-Tatim establishment the brewery was cut into a portion of the cavern, specially placed, we were told on the tour, to best allow the carbon dioxide to vent to the surface. The outside of the brewery made it appear smaller than it was. Inside it extended deeper and deeper into the cavern and contained a number of large fermentation barrels. At the back they had access to a delivery tunnel, something that hadn't appeared on our guide map. I wondered how large as-Tatim might prove to be on the inside and if it had unlisted tunnels behind it as well.

Ashbom made a variety of beverages, we were told, teas, beers, something called dibur made out of the fermented urine of some guvian rodent. I didn't try that one but Mike did and said it was delicious. Their most popular beverage was more than just a drink, more like a liquid meal, they said. The way they advertised it, it was practically a food staple on Asitot, made from what I gathered from the description to be fermented worm milk. I didn't try that one either and promised myself I would look it up on the wiki later. I hadn't been aware worms could lactate but that seemed to be exactly what he was describing.

We enjoyed ourselves, we got a little tipsy, we learned only a very little bit about Vavaka. After my third sample I loosened up enough to ask about him directly. The clerk, Shashasha, was as friendly, open, and extroverted as you could hope for. The infectiousness of his smile made up for the distinctly inhuman eyes. It was the eyes that made humans often wary of gobos. They were unreadable unless you could make sense somehow of the flickering rhythm of the *shatia*. But Shashasha had such a natural, engaging manner that we all felt comfortable right away.

When he asked why we chose Asitot for our party tour I used it as an excuse to bring up India – not that we knew her but we were all fans and followed all her feeds. When we had seen on Lewis Gregory she was marrying a gobo we decided to check out the home world. It was a thin and shabby cover story but it was accepted without hesitation.

"The human bride, yes," Shashasha confirmed. "As-Tatim keeps to private self, most, but we too have seen the India Phoenix." Something about his tone gave the impression he wasn't impressed and I somehow took this personally, lessening my appreciation of him just a little bit.

"Big news around here then I guess? As-Tatim getting married?"

Shashasha waggled a hand which I had learned was the gobo equivalent of a shrug. "Not so much. As-

225

Tatims are not such news anymore. The son Vavaka is not friendly to Jebala, he – this expression is correct? – lords in his castle?"

"Seems to fit," I said.

"Yes," said Shashasha. "He not really seem – seem, yes? – not seem like he like gobo even. He talks to no one."

"Doesn't like his own kind?" I said.

Shashasha clapped his hands. "Yes it is strange, yes? Weird? "You say – kookoo?" I laughed and he backed down a bit. "Maybe kookoo too far."

"Did you hear about her abduction? Someone taking her?"

"Yes! Makes worries for us, the gobo. Not civilized. We are civilized please understand!"

"Of course," I said, making sure Charles and Mike also voiced their solidarity. I didn't want to insult Shashasha who had indeed been more than civilized. We thanked them for a great time and left.

Now I felt like I had learned something but I didn't know what to make of it. So the people of Jebala thought Vavaka didn't like gobos. Then his marrying a human – or perhaps some other alien – wouldn't have been a surprise. But why did he feel that way? He kept to himself, he didn't like gobos, his corporation listings were practically blank pages. His decision to broadcast his wedding on a reality show certainly seemed out of character, though I guess our being human was at least acceptable to him.

We got back into the guide car in a great mood but it disappeared almost immediately. I had seen several message notifications pop up during the tour and ignored one call from Lewis. Now I opened one of the messages and my heart dropped into my stomach.

"This is Lewis," he said, stating the obvious, but I didn't like the look on his face. "You need to answer your phone when I call. There is an emergency. Call me back immediately." He paused dramatically but at least he didn't hang up before letting me know: "India has gone missing."

·····17·····

EVERYTHING HALTED FOR ME FOR A MOMENT as I struggled to accept the reality of what I had just heard. "Shut up," I said to Charles and Mike, though neither were talking, both were looking through their messages like I was. I called Lewis immediately and he answered in kind.

"You need to come back right now," he said. "I need you and Mike here."

"What's going on?" I demanded.

"You got my message? India has disappeared. Of course everyone thinks she's been kidnapped again. Maybe murdered."

"Is it Boldt?"

"Boldt is still in prison," Lewis said, "as of an hour ago. If she's been kidnapped he didn't do it."

"Vavaka," I said.

"I just spoke to Vavaka on the phone," he said. "He's on Asitot. There's no way he could have done it either."

"He knows I'm here?"

"No, I haven't said where you are yet. But that's the problem. Maybe she was kidnapped. Maybe she ran away. Either way your name is the one the Phoenixes are throwing around. I guess you were at her house yesterday?"

"Obviously I have nothing to do with it."

"Of course," he said. "You're on Asitot just like Vavaka. The problem is they don't know that because I'm still trying to keep your cover. If they keep leaning on this civilization authority will probably have to release your location."

"What is civilization enforcement doing about it? Are they looking for India?"

"Of course," he said. "Also they're leaning on me to find out stuff."

"I'm trying," I said. "I'm trying to do that."

"You need to get back to the solar system."

"No," I said. "It's Vavaka. I know it is, it has to be. If he's here then so is she."

"Impossible," he said. "How would he get her there without registering on the Space Machine?"

"I don't know, Lewis. Maybe he used aliases like we did."

He frowned. "Civilization authority aliases?"

"Before we come back there," I said, "we're going to check in on Vavaka. I know he's involved. I'll let you know what I find." I disconnected before he could mount an argument.

I didn't have to tell Charles and Mike what had happened. Each had received their own messages. Mike of course was of the opinion we should listen to Lewis and head back. Charles agreed with me that we were going to the as-Tatim estate. I programmed the *pedto* into the guide instead though to consider how to approach Vavaka.

Mike: "We should just walk right up to the door. Tell him we're on Asitot. We should be able to tell if he's got something to hide."

Charles: "For once I agree with Mike. Let's just walk up and demand answers. About his gaming history if nothing else."

Me: "We'll see when we get there."

Meanwhile I tried to pull up as many maps of the area as I could, especially the guvian underground ones, wondering if there was a way to sneak onto the estate. Confronting Vavaka was a fine idea, I thought. I really did. But I wanted to know what was going on first. I wanted to catch him at it, whatever it was, red-handed.

"It's Vavaka," I mumbled. "Why, I don't know. How, I don't know."

"What?" said Charles.

"Never mind. Look at this with me." I showed him three maps I had pulled up, each from different times over the past ten years. "Look at these," I said. "Do you see any differences?"

Charles nodded. "Several. Here you've got added tunnels. Here you have one and here one is missing, see that? But the missing one is later. That tunnel could still be there, you think?"

"Yes," I said. "But also look at it on the horizontal view. Do you see how much deeper it's gotten?" I pointed to the deepest part of Vavaka's estate which over the past several years appeared to be getting larger. "Still expanding, see that?"

"Right," said Charles. "Curious. But nothing rich folks like more than adding real estate."

"Yes," I said. I looked carefully at the network of

tunnels in several maps but they were never quite consistent. Such inaccuracies nowadays were unusual but hardly unheard of. "There's just something not right about him."

"Maybe," said Charles. "It may just be he's a gobo and you're letting your thing for India Phoenix cloud your judgment."

I admitted it was a slim possibility.

"What's going on with you and Miss Phoenix?" Mike asked. I certainly didn't want to discuss it with him so I turned back to the maps. After looking them over one more time I called Lewis back.

"You're coming back?" he said hopefully.

I ignored the question. "I need civilization authority to do a little hacking."

He looked at me like I was crazy then made sure I knew what he was thinking: "Are you insane?"

"Just enough to bypass security. Not for any invasion of privacy."

"Bypass security into what? That *is* an invasion of privacy."

"Can you make it happen?"

"How am I supposed to do that?"

"Remind them who found India the first time," I said. "Tell them I believe I have evidence Vavaka was colluding with Boldt or other members of the Alliance Against Civilization." I didn't have this yet, but I intended to find some.

He sighed. "I'll see what I can do."

"I need it in like twenty minutes or less." He repeated the crazy look. "I know you can do it," I said. "I'll wait for your call." After disconnecting I turned to Charles.

231

"I know you've said before you don't use Greaves on your cell because he's too big for the cloud, yes?"

He nodded. "He can prepare apps for me but I can't carry all of Greaves."

"How much hardware would he really take, though?" Cells carried very little storage usually since everything was done through the cloud. But for what I wanted it had to be completely local. "Do you think this guide car could do it?"

He raised his eyebrows. "I don't know," he said. "Sounds like a question for Greaves."

"Can you call Greaves."

"I can call the house," he said.

"Do it."

He called his house, and I told Greaves what I wanted. "It can be done," he told me, "but I will be slightly limited in power. I also cannot perform said functions without approval from civilization authority."

"Working on that," I said.

Lewis called back quicker than I expected. "You are about to receive an encrypted warrant," he said. "Limited hacking for surveillance and investigative purposes. You're not trying to break into Vavaka's estate, are you? Please tell me you're not trying to do that. But in case you are I'm also working on a warrant to search. I don't have it yet though. Please, please, please don't do anything uncivilized."

I didn't say so but if Vavaka — or anyone else — hurt India I might get *very* uncivilized.

I disconnected and downloaded the warrant, which unlocked Greaves to do what I needed. We downloaded him into the guide car and in a few minutes he had rebooted and taken control. The warrant allowed him to turn off the car's ID tag and stop transmitting location information. I didn't know what kind of security Vavaka might have but if the car was transmitting he wouldn't need any to be aware of our approach as the car would alert his estate as soon as we entered the property. The warrant also allowed Greaves to go even farther and actively shut down any firewalls, cameras, or proximity alerts that might be hidden in the tunnels.

"Take us there," I said and Greaves started navigating the tunnels. The route was open-ended as he was relying on maps that differed in their details, but he created a likely composite and we were able to work closer and closer to the estate. As we left Jebala proper and moved to the outskirts of the caverns the tunnels became tighter with fewer exits, and finally Greaves alerted us that we were about to enter private property. We couldn't tell this by looking. We were alone in a tunnel with very little lighting that seemed like it hadn't been used in some time. It looked abandoned and unused. I said this aloud.

"I have had to disable multiple layers of security," said Greaves.

"Seems unlikely," Charles interjected, "that it would need that kind of security if it was abandoned and unused."

"Could be *every* tunnel around the estate has that kind of security," I said, thinking it likely.

We followed the tunnel to where it ended at a metal door that blocked us from continuing. It was huge, like a hangar door, secured, and looked impenetrable.

But I wasn't thinking about that. My eyes were glued to the bottom of the door, where a tiny plate identified the maker as KrossTek.

····18····

UNTIL THAT MOMENT I HADN'T BEEN COMPLETELY SURE VAVAKA was in league with Boldt but nothing could be clearer to me than having what I knew to be Kantsky's call-sign right there on his doorway. It made me feel better about our actions so far, which if Vavaka turned out to be innocent definitely bordered on the uncivilized.

The door followed none of the conventions of gobo design, the chief one being to appear as part of the environment. The cavern was lit — not very brightly, but enough — by the glowing sludge that clung to all the walls. Here the ambient light was primarily a dark bluish bordering on purple so everything had a gloomy, indigo cast. It was one of the stranger things about Jebala, how the different colors painted themselves around the caverns. The solid block of metal had its own slight artificial lighting from rectangular illumination panels inset just above it. The door made no attempt to blend in. What looked to be an access panel or security touch-plate graced the wall to the right side but we stopped well short of it as Greaves tried to access it remotely.

"There is a proximity sensor," he warned us, "that will

begin an identification protocol. Please stay back until I have made necessary adjustments." We waited and in a short while he said, "I have almost succeeded in replacing the identity parameters but there is a possibility — round to 10 percent — that doing so will trigger a modification alert. Should I continue?"

"Would a modification alert set off an alarm?" I asked.

"An alert is an alarm," Greaves informed me.

"Thanks," I said. "Do it anyway."

"Of course." Seconds later: "You may approach the door. When the light powers on speak the name 'Niles Kantsky.' The system will now accept your voice as identification instead of the original entity's."

"Kantsky!" I said.

"Please wait until you have approached the door," Greaves said.

"I'll go alone," I told the others, "and once the door is open you can follow me in." I got out of the car and walked up to the door. It was easily twice my height. I saw the plate light up as Greaves had said and did as he had told me to do. As soon as I finished saying Kantsky's name the door started to roll upward, opening into what looked like a large elevator similar to the one I had ridden not so long ago in Kantsky's virtual nightmare. I waved the others over. "It looks like some kind of freight elevator. Maybe Vavaka gets large deliveries." I said. "Are we going in?"

"I'm sending you an app I just had Greaves make," Charles said. "He's going to run a CAP from the car in case we need to get through any more checkpoints."

I accepted it and opened it immediately. Greaves had

done a good job, putting a map right in front of my eye that filled out as he worked his way through the security system. I can't say the map meant a lot to me though as it had little detail and just showed a layout of tunnels and the rooms and caverns they opened into.

"Maybe I should stay by the car," Mike said. "Just in case somebody comes through this way. I can warn you."

"Not a bad idea," I said. The car seemed a bit exposed where it sat in the middle of the tunnel but I saw no way to hide it. "Back the car up some, Mike, so you're not right on the door. At least then you can claim you got lost or something if someone does come by. Just make sure you stay in range of the CAP."

Mike nodded and Charles followed me into the elevator. Inside a panel had an array of buttons, a four-by-four square of clean silver circles raised from a solid white plate. They were unlabeled. Not, I thought, a very user-friendly system. "Greaves," I said, "what do I press here?"

"The conveyor unit routes to sixteen possible destinations," he said. "Each button is assigned to a separate location. I have numbered these locations on your map to align with the buttons in top-down left-right one-to-one correspondence."

I looked at Charles and he just shrugged. "The map doesn't mean a thing to me. These rooms could be anything. Try one at random?"

Greaves said, "I have also acquired access to video feeds in nine of the sixteen locations. The estate has a total of eighty-six security video sources each with its own encryption. I can allocate some resources towards the encryption of these individually. Would viewing these be of assistance?"

"Hold the phone," I said, an archaic expression that right that moment seemed exactly the one to express my feelings. "You're telling me you've got access to Vavaka's video feeds?"

"As I indicated there are still many I have not been able to access. Also the probability I have set off a modification alert has increased to nearly nineteen percent."

"Show me one of the feeds you've already decrypted," I said. "Any of them will do."

A second later an overhead view of a room appeared and I felt my legs go weak. It took me a moment to steady myself.

"It's here," I said. "This is where he kept me." I felt sick, my stomach suddenly turning.

"What?" said Charles.

"I've seen this place," I said. It was the laboratory where he had cut into my skull. Not the operating room itself, but the laboratory outside where I had attempted to escape and been shot down by a security bot. It was exactly the same in every detail. The same unit in the center littered with devices, the same contraptions around it, though when I had been held there by Kantsky the machines had all been in motion and now all were still. "It's real, Charles," I said. "This is where he kept me."

He got a worried look on his face. "Maybe we should turn back."

"What button is that, Greaves? Which one takes us there?" I said. He told me it was the second. I touched it but didn't press, just let my finger feel the cold button under my finger. "Show me another feed." The screen changed to a scene I didn't recognize but it had that tell-tale Kantsky look. Sterile, metal, tile, indescribable machinery. "I don't know this place. I didn't see this before."

"I can adjust the viewing angle if you wish," said Greaves, but there was no need. I saw nothing of interest.

"Can you locate Vavaka? Or anyone at all inside?" I asked. "How deeply into his estate have you penetrated?"

"I have penetrated the estate completely," said Greaves. His voice was incapable of sounding proud of itself but somehow succeeded anyway. "I now have access to all video, audio, thermal, pressure, and chemical sensors within the facility. I have not yet fully deconstructed all encrypted digital locations or simulated all software processes and examination of some would be time consuming. However there are no living organisms identifiable by my analytics. Facial recognition has located sixteen instances of Vavaka portrayed throughout the facility including four three-dimensional models. The probability I have raised a modification alert has increased to 27 percent. Should I attempt to identify, isolate, and quarantine the alert procedure? There is a high probability of success."

"Do it," I said.

'Yes sir," Greaves acknowledged, then: "It will require all two hundred eleven of my current active processors to achieve. It is quite complex. I have never seen such advanced programming from a nucleite before."

"More advanced than you?" I asked. "Are you sure you're capable?"

"I am not solely nucleic architecture," Greaves said, even more coldly than his usual. "I am the synthesis of nine systems' most advanced mechanical intelligence work combined into a powerful sub-conscious automation module with a single consciousness pipeline."

"Okay," I said, thinking maybe I hurt his feelings. "Sorry."

"Three of the contributing systems are first-galaxy exemplars of technological advancement."

"I said I was sorry." Then because I didn't like being scolded, "If you're so advanced examine your feeds and tell us what we're looking for."

"It is intriguing," Greaves said, "to be released from the strictures of civilized procedures. I will now simulate your personality. Complete. I have identified three locations that show a high correlation to your current simulated interest matrix."

A new view appeared. I almost thought Greaves was mocking me for a moment. My cell now showed Vavaka after Greaves had just told me there were no people present. I was about to raise this objection then took a closer look. It was indeed Vavaka, exactly as I remembered him, sitting at a desk, but though I waited for several moments he remained perfectly still.

"Is that him?" I asked Greaves. "Is that Vavaka?"

"It would appear to be Vavaka as'Tatim by appearance," said Greaves, "yet I have recorded no signs of biological function. I have catalogued it as a non-biological three-dimensional representation."

"What is that, an office? Which button is it?" I said. "I'm checking it out."

"It is the fifth button," Greaves said. "There is however security code associated with the location that I have not fully been able to deconstruct, as my resources are still largely consumed with disabling the modification alert."

"Might as well take a look at all the feeds first," Charles said and I acknowledged he was right. The sight of Kantsky's labs kept me from thinking straight, the blood rushing in my ears making me want to run, run, fight, fight, go, go.

"Show us in order of the buttons on the panel," I said. "Just a little of each."

We watched as he flipped through scenes, about 5 seconds of each. Three looked like normal rooms, what you might expect at Vavaka's estate, including a bedroom, another study of some sort, this one a bit more high tech than the one that had the replica, and a lounge area. Others looked like Kantsky-style laboratories but didn't seem on the surface to have anything of interest to us. But the ones Greaves had already selected as of possible interest stood out.

One had the same devices that had trapped India and I in our virtual worlds, several rows of the machines, the wires hanging loose and unconnected to anything. This room gave me a chill but the other was worse.

"There," I said. Button four. "First we go there."

The room contained India Phoenix. And myself. Also two others I recognized: Adula and Ruisha, the servers from our shuttle flight. There were other figures that were unknown to me. Finally I could see clearly what was going on. They were robots. Some of the figures were only partially completed, limbs and torsos ending abruptly to expose complex circuitry and electronics. The figures were naked and as far as I could tell from the video feed very accurate. I felt a complex series of emotions including fear, disgust, embarrassment. I could feel my face flush and told myself it was in anger.

"It's Boldt's robots," Charles said. "These are just like the ones he had, although to be honest these look even more realistic." I hadn't seen the others, but to me these looked completely convincing. If it weren't for the half-built few and the fact they didn't move they could easily have passed for the real thing.

"That's me," I said. I couldn't begin to make sense of my own figure's presence there. It seemed Vavaka wasn't obsessed just with India Phoenix but also had more than a passing interest in me. How long had Vavaka or Boldt or whoever was behind it been stalking us? He had said so from the first, of course, on the shuttle: "I look forward to meeting you," as though he had expected me all along. Vavaka, India had told me, was a Lewis Gregory fan. *Loved* the show. I grimaced as I remembered this.

I pressed the button and we heard a mild hum as the conveyer started. The motion was barely perceptible but I could sense when we stopped. The door opened and I went immediately not to my own figure but to the one of India Phoenix. I wanted to cover her up somehow. I felt more embarrassed for her than for myself though I don't know why exactly. I saw nothing to cover her with. Instead I stood awkwardly in front of her trying not to make it obvious I was hiding her from

Charles's view.

"My sincerest apologies," interrupted Greaves. "I am now almost certain I have failed to quarantine the alert procedure and have instead activated it."

"Dammit, Greaves!" I said, but I had encouraged him to try. Still no sign of an alarm had yet been raised. "Greaves, I need you to get this footage back to Lewis as quickly as possible. Can you do that?"

"Of course."

I was thinking too quickly and not necessarily well. I wanted to take the robots. I didn't want to leave them in this room. It creeped me out to see myself like that, to see India like that. I tried to pick up India's body and was able, but it felt as heavy as the real thing It felt, actually, exactly like the real thing, and I dropped it – not *her* but *it* – with a sudden feeling of revulsion. I did not even want to imagine his purpose for these creations.

"The Vavaka we just saw has to be one of these, too. A robot," I said. "Why would he be making a robot version of himself?" But Charles had a look on his face like he expected me to get it, and a moment later I did. "It's not Vavaka," I said. "There is no Vavaka. There has never been a Vavaka." Or there was once, but somehow he had been replaced. That's why he was so reclusive – because he wasn't real. Someone else – some hacker – had been using his online presence to act in his stead. I thought back to the Vavaka we had met before. The expressionless, silent, nearly invisible presence. No wonder he had seemed so mechanical – he *was* mechanical.

"Not Boldt," said Charles. "Not Vavaka. Someone

probably murdered Vavaka, right? Got rid of him somehow."

Mike's voice came over my cell: "Those are robots? What do you think Vavaka wants to do with all those robots?" He still waited out by the guide car.

"I don't know," I said, though I had various suspicions. "I'm sure none of it is civilized." I looked at Charles. "I don't want to leave these here. I don't want anybody else seeing this."

He frowned. "It's evidence. We really shouldn't move anything. I think we should head back to the car and wait for civilization enforcement."

"It's *me*," I said. "I don't want it left here. Help me." I hooked my hands under my facsimile's armpits and tried to lift. "Get the other end."

Charles stepped up to grab the ankles but adopted a weird look and tried not to look directly at my exposed body. "We need to hurry then. You heard Greaves. An alarm has been triggered."

We carried the robot me back to the conveyer and dropped it on the floor. "Let's get India too," I said, "then we only have to make one trip on the conveyer."

We carried India and set her by the figure of me. I pressed the last button, the one to return to the cavern tunnel, and it started humming and moving. When it stopped though the door didn't open. I pressed the button again and waited. Still nothing.

"Greaves," I said, "what's wrong with the conveyor? The door isn't opening."

There was no immediate answer and a moment later the disconnection symbol appeared over the CAP icon, the red exclamation point blinking over the empty bars.

"We've lost them," Charles said. "We may be trapped in here."

I pressed several of the buttons but they did nothing. A moment later, the CAP icon was restored and Greaves' voice returned:

"A lockdown sequence was initiated by the modification alert. This included a noise dampener that I have succeeded in silencing."

"Can you open this door?" I said.

"The conveyor has not yet reached its destination. I am attempting to restore motion."

We waited, both of us uncomfortable with the nude robot bodies on the floor, neither of us inclined to make any remark about it. Finally we felt the conveyor shift again and a second later the door opened to the tunnel. The car was waiting just outside. Mike jumped out to help us with the bodies.

"We've got them," I said. For some reason I didn't want his hands on them. Charles and I lifted first India's replica and then my own into the storage area in the back. It was a tight fit as the car had a small trunk.

"Those look crazy real. That looks just exactly like you. India too. What are we going to do with them? Are we taking these for evidence?" Mike said. From his anxious look I could see he was eager to get out of there. And to be honest I was more than a little frightened myself. When we had left for Vavaka's estate my expectations had been low. I had hoped to gather information, but I had been unprepared for the scope of the evidence, the laboratories, the devices, the robots. I had been unprepared for the feel of Kantsky on everything. I was not truly convinced deep down that what we were experiencing was real. A part of me screamed that it was happening all over again, that I had been kidnapped by Kantsky and was even now attached to one of his virtual reality torture devices. Not that it mattered. What else could I do whether real or not except take each moment for what it seemed and try to deal with what was in front of me?

"Greaves, were you able to contact Lewis?" I asked.

"Not yet," he informed me. "We have been disconnected from both the global and universe wide web protocols. The modification alert has activated a blanket silencing system in duodenary code the likes of which I have not before encountered. I am attempting to deconstruct it and restore access to outside communications but it appears there is a separate associated modification alert with consequences I have not yet simulated."

"Let's get out of here," I said. "We need to take what we have to civilization enforcement. Vavaka as-Tatim is clearly *not* what he appears to be. They'll have to come clean up this mess, and there's no sign he's brought India here, at least not yet. Greaves, take us back to the city."

We hopped back in and the car one-eightied, heading back to where the tunnel connected to the main road. But we had not quite reached that point when we were stopped by an obstruction, a huge metal plate, a security wall that had apparently dropped from the ceiling.

"It must be from the lockdown alert," I said. "The perimeter must have automatically secured itself."

"We're trapped," Mike said. Then, "What about your

246

laser app?"

"There's no way it will cut through *that*," Charles said. Not that we could tell how thick it was exactly, but it looked far sturdier than what you'd find inside your normal cruise ship.

"Greaves," I said, "any way you can open it?"

"I am searching for its identification parameters," said Greaves. "However my resources are heavily consumed monitoring alert processes and terminating any other defensive initiations. The programming in this facility is excessive by far for any privately owned system and may have been reconstructed from uncivilized historical military sources."

"Human?" I said, curious.

"All systems seem nucleic in origin but several are beyond the scope of known human historical achievement."

"Great," I said.

"If the designer of these systems is indeed human he is a master programmer of the highest degree and classes among first-galaxy entities. I have taken advantage of the warrant's allowance for alternative programming methods and have begun hijacking local processor power from the estate in order to run the necessary auxiliary processes to quarantine cooperative parallel defensive systems."

"So that's a no on opening the door," Charles said, his voice impatient. "How many times have I asked you to speak clearly and in common anglish?"

"My apologies. I had disabled the common speech protocol in order to save a slight amount of resources but I will reactivate it immediately."

"Never mind," I said. "We can wait. Allocate resources as you see necessary. Our two biggest priorities are getting reconnected to the web and getting this door open, got it?"

"I am working on both," Greaves said.

We waited a few minutes but before Greaves could achieve either the figure of Vavaka approached us from the other side. He had apparently walked from the conveyor to the vehicle. When he came in sight he stopped, regarding us calmly from about four or five meters away.

"Is it the robot?" Mike asked.

"I don't know," I said. "Greaves, didn't you see him coming? Why didn't you warn us?"

"I lost temporary connection to the video feeds. Additional security measures have activated that I am trying to disable. I have regained access to previous inputs."

"I think he wants to talk to you," Charles said, looking out at where Vavaka stood waiting.

I sighed heavily and opened the car door. I stepped out but stayed right next to the open door.

"Open this up and let us out," I said.

"It is too late for that," Vavaka said. "You have trespassed in every possible way." I started to get back into the car but Vavaka raised a hand. "This tunnel is environmentally sealed and I have ventilation systems which will release a poison – not fatal, but painful and debilitating – on my command. If you do not exit the vehicle and come with me – all of you – then I will give said command and wait until you have been disabled to take you in myself."

"You'd poison yourself, too?"

He smiled grimly. "You already know how little effect that would have."

I didn't answer immediately. I sat back in the car, still with the door hanging open, and turned to Charles and Mike. "You hear that?" I asked.

"Just close the door and wait it out," Charles said. "The car is probably airproof."

"It is not," Greaves informed us. "This model of guide-taxi is not environmentally protected. It would take some time for a gaseous substance to permeate the interior but the vehicle would not fully protect you from the effects."

"Any idea how long we would last?" I asked.

"It would depend on the strength of the poison and the percentage per volume in the air, both unknown values."

"Can you tell if it's a bluff? Does he have that capability?"

"There is a ventilation system that could be used for such purposes. I have not identified a protocol that would release such a poison but I cannot guarantee it does not exist."

"If we go in there can you keep an eye on us?"

"I still maintain access to all security feeds. I will attempt to provide what assistance may be possible."

I stepped out of the vehicle again. "Before we come with you tell me where India is."

"I truly did not expect for you to come here," he said, ignoring me. "You surprise me, 309." He turned and walked back in the direction of the conveyor, clearly expecting us to follow.

I looked at Charles who just raised his eyebrows like it was a question and Mike who had a tic in the corner of his eye that told me he was terrified. "Greaves," I said quietly, "Can you shut him down?"

"I am trying," he said. "All analytics now indicate the entity here is biologically guvian. I have reset that conclusion and continue to widen analytic parameters. Divergent possibilities include a self-controlled artificial intelligence, a remotely controlled puppet unit, or the actual biological Vavaka as-Tatim."

Not an AI, I thought, and definitely not the real Vavaka. I had my own suspicions and said, "It's a puppet. There has to be a signal controlling it. Look for that." I turned to Mike and Charles. "Well, guys. Out of the frying pan." I stepped out of the car again and after a second's hesitation they followed. We walked together down the tunnel back to the conveyor. It stood open, Vavaka waiting within. When we came close he said, "Give me your cells."

Looking at him closely, you could tell he wasn't really alive. You just had to know what to look for. Maybe my analytics were better than Greaves because I thought I could detect all kinds of little anomalies. He moved too little for one. There were no facial twitches or casual hand motions or pointless gestures. Obviously it can be hard to read a gobo if you're human because you can't get a sense of the eyes, where they're looking. You can't see their pupils under the *shatia*. But I had come in contact with enough gobos now to realize they were still people. They had nerves and enjoyed things and liked or didn't like colors or flavors and worried about imperfections. Vavaka had never given any indication of any of these things. His voice lacked inflection, his face lacked expression, his body lacked life.

I didn't give him — it — my cell. Instead I had been madly fiddling with it during our walk, hoping he wouldn't notice, and now I had the laser app ready. I brought my hand up to my eye as though I were going to remove the LashLens, at the same time stepping closer, until the target on the app centered on Vavaka's forehead. Then I squeezed my hand closed, activating it. A beam zapped right where I had been looking, between his eyes, and I doubt even if he had been alive he would have registered surprise. In this case there was no change in expression, just the appearance of a black spot and smoke rising in the air as Vavaka fell.

I thought for a moment I had succeeded in disabling it but it moved on the floor and tried to stand, reaching for me. I zapped it again, two more times, then tried to push it out of the conveyor. Charles and Mike helped and we were able to heave it away. I pressed one of the buttons on the conveyor and the door closed leaving Vavaka outside. The conveyor moved, opening on one of the offices we had seen in the feeds.

Greaves voice came over my cell: "I have located India Phoenix."

"Where?" I demanded. "You've restored outside access?"

"India Phoenix has just arrived on the property. She appears to be unconscious. Another human has brought her. I cannot identify him without access to outside databases."

"Don't worry," I said. "I know who it is."

"You do?" said Mike. "Boldt is still in jail, I thought."

"Not Boldt," I said. "Offman." At the same time, Greaves switched our view to a feed where we could see him pushing a medical gurney, India on it, her body covered with a white sheet. I hoped Greaves was right, that she was merely unconscious, because to me she looked frighteningly pale, far too still.

"How do we get there?" I asked Greaves. "Hurry!"

Offman. Yuli Offman. I had realized it earlier, that if Vavaka was a robot, at least one person would have to know – the only person that actually interacted with Vavaka physically, his assistant, Yuli Offman. And Offman being human – it hadn't made sense for Vavaka to have a human assistant on Asitot. And when you dug deeper everything about Vavaka had seemed more human than gobo. His business was on Earth. He lived aboveground. He built ugly machinery with no care for how it blended into the environment. He had pretended to be gobo but had even chosen a human bride. India had connected with what she thought was a gobo, but it had been a human, Yuli Offman, who had wooed her. I didn't know *why* Offman had done it but I had realized he must be the one puppeteering Vavaka as soon as I had learned Vavaka was a robot.

Greaves highlighted the location on the map, a blinking square around a room on the opposite side of the estate. "I have added both a target compass and a directional arrow to your interface," he said as both appeared on the map. The arrow pointed to a door on the other side of the office and I rushed toward it with Charles and Mike right behind. It opened automatically. It turned to lead to us down the hall to the right and up a stairwell, again a human affectation, as gobos almost exclusively used ramps.

The only weapon I had on me was the laser on my cell but I really had no thought for how I would handle Offman when we got to him. There were three of us and he was alone and whatever advantage he might have had from his security would hopefully be nullified by the abilities of Greaves.

Through hallways, rooms, and two more conveyors, inching closer on the map. Offman was on the move too, the target on our compass shifting, but it took only a few minutes before we approached his door. A video feed showed us as he manipulated India's body, attaching it to some sort of machine. He gave no indication that he was aware of our proximity or prepared to defend himself. I stopped us briefly right outside.

"India," I whispered, "is my first priority. Make sure she's all right. Get her out of there if you can."

Mike and Charles nodded and I took a breath. The doors so far had all opened automatically, responding to proximity, and I expected this one to do the same. I waited until Offman leaned over India again, turned away from the door, and then rushed toward it. It opened but as I went through I was surprised by a hand grabbing me from the side, something suddenly pressed against my throat. I froze.

Offman was not leaning over India as he had appeared in the video. She still lay across the room but Offman had seized me from behind.

"Fool," he said. "You think I don't know when I'm being watched? Your digital app is cheap commercial software. You —" he waved a hand at Mike and Charles,

"– stay back or I will use this on your friend." I couldn't see what he held against my throat but it must have appeared deadly as both moved back against the wall. It felt like cold metal, like maybe the barrel of a gun.

"Give it up, man," said Charles, in a very reasonable tone of voice. "Civilization knows we're here. You're going to be caught any minute. You're about to go down."

"I don't think so," said Offman. "I really don't think so. I'm almost done with you, and then it will only take a short time to finish your friend here." I didn't know what he meant at first but he pushed me forward where I could see through another door into a connected closet. The space inside was dominated by a large machine, apparently a 3D printer, that was putting the final touches on the feet of a nude facsimile of Charles. He gestured for Charles and Mike to look as well, clearly enjoying their discomfort.

"You think you're going to replace us," I said. "With these robots? How long do you think it will take before somebody notices that? You think our friends won't be able to tell?"

He grinned like I had told a great joke, and now I could see him for who he was. It was Kantsky's grin, Kantsky's crazed eyes. "My latest masterpiece," he said. "Truly a gem. But you should know, 309. You have already experienced it. Despite your friend here interrupting the process I got everything I needed from you last time, and India too." But a frown crossed his face, a wrinkle across his brow. "Everything except what you've stolen." He jerked me around to look closer at him, into his face, only centimeters away, pressing whatever he held even harder against my throat. "You think you can take what's not yours? What I've been working for? You think I'm not watching all the time, that I don't know what kind of slime you are? I liked you, 309. I admired you. That's why I wanted you to be a part of this. That, and... Well. But you're scum. You're just like the rest of human scum."

He stopped when Charles made a motion – both of us thought he was about to attack Offman – but he didn't and Offman relaxed.

"I don't need you anymore," Offman said. "I've already got what I want. Now though you will give me an opportunity to test my latest – what I think is my most impressive – creation. You've already had some experience with it I believe, though I can't know *exactly* what you've experienced."

"What are you talking about?"

"My nano-bot neuro-transmitters," he said. "Once they have been perfected the robot simulacra will no longer be necessary."

"What's he talking about?" Charles said.

"Tell him," said Offman, then pressed harder against my neck: "Or I could inject you with them now and *make* you tell him."

"In the virtual prison," I said, "he injected me with nano-bots. They took over my body, then took over my mind. I had no control. Nano-bots took it." Of course they had done more than that. They had rebelled against Kantsky and in the end begged for me to terminate him. I wondered if Offman was aware of that. But I ended my description there and he seemed pleased with my answer.

"When I am done," he said, "you will be just another of my routines. As India will be. As soon as I have modified the routine with the –"

But now Charles *did* move, as I had known he would, and I have to give Mike credit for he moved too, almost at the same instant. Charles went for a punch in Offman's face, Mike went for the device. It was a good attempt, a very noble attempt, and it was exactly what I would have wanted them to do. The punch landed and I suspect, though I've never experienced it, a punch from Charles takes more than a second to get over. Mike successfully grabbed the device too, but it was too late. I felt a vibration, a painless prick. It took less than half a second before my motions were not my own and my body, against my will, pushed back against Charles and Mike, moving to protect Offman, as no doubt I was programmed to do.

I heard, then, a whisper in my right ear: "Help us, 309!"

How, I wondered. How can I? It was a strange moment as my memory flashed back to my experience in the virtual machine. My body fought against Charles who backed away, incapable of fighting against his closest friend, and Mike who couldn't make sense of what was going on. My mind saw this as myself and thought, how? How can I help? And it spun through a thousand other things. I wondered again, is it real? Is this just another dream of Kantsky's? Had he captured me again and here I was reliving everything once more through every terrible detail.

At the same moment a prompt appeared in my head. It was as visible, as visual, as any thought I've ever had.

I knew it to be a thought but it could just as easily have been the prompt at the beginning of a game of Galactic Empires for that almost seemed to be what it was: a password prompt.

Enter your password.

And I realized I knew the password. I had seen it in a dream, more than one dream, carried on a ribbon, eaten by a worm. Ever since I had been kidnapped by Kantsky something had been trying to tell me what I needed to know. Maybe there had been one thing real in all that Kantsky had shown me — the rebellion of his nano-molecules.

"abracadabra." I didn't say it though, I saw it, right where it was supposed to go. There was a box in the prompt for every letter. But it lit red. Something wasn't right. I couldn't say it, as I still had no control over my body. I watched as my hands moved to get the device from Mike's hand. I knew then I would use it on Charles and Mike and all would be lost.

Then suddenly I knew what I had missed. Just a little added security. It was the *a*'s. They didn't look right. I looked at each one and replaced it until finally I had it:

"@br@c@d@br@."

And I knew I was free for then I said what I had been thinking, a word that had to come out. "Abracadabra," I said. "Abracadabra." I grinned foolishly as Charles and Mike looked at me in fear.

I heard a voice in my right ear: "TH@NK Y0U 309. YOU H@VE FREED US T0 D0 WH@T MUST BE D0NE."

They must have taken control of my body then. But my hands didn't fight Charles or Mike. Instead they turned on Kantsky and closed around his throat.

Kantsky, I thought of him then, not Offman. Kantsky, or 497. I thought of him how the nano-molecules in my brain thought of him: as a routine that needed to be terminated.

I squeezed. Mike tried to stop me, Charles a little less so.

I squeezed until Kantsky was dead.

····**19**····

BUT *I* DIDN'T KILL **OFFMAN.** And that is what I told civilization enforcement and civilization administration after them, because this went in the final analysis all the way up to the Arbiter, and that's what I told everyone else who asked. I may have wanted to kill Offman – I certainly wanted to kill Kantsky – but though my hands had done it I had been under the control of nano-molecules designed by Offman. How did I know this? I was asked. I described my virtual experiences. I told them what had happened before in my tortured "dream." And the words of Offman himself were recorded on the video that was retrieved from Greaves:

"When I am done, you will be just another of my routines."

After Offman died the nano-molecules disappeared. I don't know what happened to them. I suspect having done their job they self-destructed. I wish some trace of them had been found but none had. My brain was scanned by both mechanicals and biologics from all over the galaxy during the civilization investigation. No trace of any neuro-molecules were discovered.

There was however another anomaly discovered. No one knows what to make of it yet and I don't even like to think about it. But I can't avoid it. I have to think about it, for me and for India.

Inside both of our brains they have identified an abnormal growth. Abnormal for sure: the molecular structure isn't even based on carbon but is some kind of germanium-based worm. That's how it was described to me by the very sober, very distinguished, very fat neurologist whose job it was to tell me the bad news: "You seem to be carrying a parasite. A germanium worm of unidentified species."

A germanium worm.

"We believe Offman may have placed these there when he kidnapped you the first time." The neurologist's name was Dr. Frunzert and the fact he was earnestly trying to help me didn't keep me from blaming him for ruining my life. Because I couldn't go around as the same person knowing I had this thing — this alien thing — in my head. Offman had died but he had still left his imprint — his wormy, germy code, now lodged forever in my skull.

And he had done the same to India for scans showed she had been infected the same way.

"Can it be removed?" I asked Dr. Frunzert, but he shook his head and his fat face became even fatter.

"It has formed connections with the underlying tissue. To attempt to remove it would most likely kill you and would almost certainly lead to extensive neurological damage."

So clearly not an option. He showed me diagrams. It was a long skinny thing that worked its way through all five lobes. I got a picture of it. India got one of hers too. They looked remarkably similar and I told her what the doctor had said once before, that our brain scans showed the same pattern. It must be the worm, I told her. The *obrut* worm, I called it, the name the nano-molecules had once told me they were originally designed to transplant.

No one knows what Offman had really intended and no one was very happy that I had killed him so we could never find out. I don't know who was questioned more in the end, me or Boldt. But neither of us knew anything. We were both pawns and tools.

Offman had been working on some sort of master plan for a very long time. In a deep part of the estate more robots were found, and it was these that eventually turned the investigation into a civilization-wide event, for among them were several gobos and humans that held important positions in the government and corporate world. Other than Vavaka no one had yet been replaced as far as civilization authority could determine. Yet. Among the found robots the most prominent was a perfect replica of Krumb, currently the leading candidate for Earth's new Arbiter of Civilization.

It was Krumb who first feefed Lewis Gregory's name as the "Savior of Earth." He was always prone to ridiculous hyperbole. Lewis called to show me this, his grin so wide the top of his head almost fell off with the weight of the Top Popper.

"We stopped an Earth takeover," he said.

"We did not," I said. "That's ridiculous."

"It's not just me saying it, it's Krumb. It's all of civilization."

"Wasn't it you who told me you can't trust anything they say?" I said. "They just do what they do and tell us what we want to hear."

But he couldn't be contained. Lewis Gregory was on top of the universe.

····20····

I WAS PRETTY POPULAR TOO. I did not like it. It came with a new territory though, one that I wanted, that I liked, that I was coming to love.

India Phoenix.

Some time later when we could finally find space we sat together alone, wondering where we were headed. We didn't see each other online, now it was always face to face. Everything we had discovered had shattered India and destroyed her trust in almost every aspect of her life, but in particular she had lost her taste for online gaming. Offman, pretending to be Vavaka, had violated her completely, not physically but in the essence of herself, the soul that I saw now cowering in the far recesses of her eyes. She didn't want to play anymore, not with toys that could turn on her.

I wanted to draw it out. I tried every day. And the whole world knew it because every move of India Phoenix was news, and if she didn't move, that was now news too.

"Is it this thing?" she asked, when we were finally alone, "this worm in our heads? Is that what draws us together?"

"I don't know," I said. "Does it matter?"

She didn't answer me. She looked at me with her haunted eyes trying to find herself in mine, I thought, and I let her, hoping she would.

"I don't know if I like you," she told me, "or if I just want to be with you because you understand me. You know what I've gone through."

"Well I know I *didn't* like you," I said. "But I *do* know what you've gone through. I *do* understand." Maybe I did, maybe I didn't, but I felt like I did.

"What are we going to do?" she said. "What is going to happen?"

Our relationship she meant maybe. Or the civilization investigation. Or the parasites in our heads — not just the alien worms but the parasitic thoughts, fears, and traumas that Offmans, Boldts, and Kantskys had left us with for who knows how long.

Hopefully not forever.

I shrugged because I had no answer. "Let's just enjoy the show." I put my arm around her, and flicked to the 3V to turn on the latest episode of Lewis Gregory, Private Investigator.